THE LEGEND OF TUG FEST
AND OTHER LECLAIRE GHOST STORIES

Edited by Ellen Tsagaris

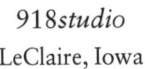

918*studio*
LeClaire, Iowa

The Legend of Tug Fest and Other LeClaire Ghost Stories
Edited by Ellen Tsagaris

140 pages
Published by 918*studio*
Isbn 0985194413
Isbn 13 978-0-9851944-1-3

Copyright © 2012 Buffalo Bill Museum, LeClaire

Printed in the United States of America
All rights reserved

"The Past" is from *The Citadel of Thought* published in 1917 by Linotype Composition Company, Davenport, Iowa

Cover and interior design by Rivertown Creative

100% of the proceeds from the sale of this collection support the Buffalo Bill Museum of LeClaire, Iowa

The Past

Mary Eveline Parkhurst

The past has gone in rapid flight
In the wake of day and of night;
The shadows and sunshine had play
In each fleeting and passing day;
So grief, toil, anxiety and care
Crushed many a soul in despair.
Many drank in careless leisure
From the sparkling cup of pleasure.

"Gone forever," moans from the past
Like a dying wintery blast;
We do not hear the crushing tread
Nor the sighing of hearts that bled.
In Memory's castle most fair
A soothing radiance dwells there;
For choice pictures are on the wall
That come from the past at our call.

—*LeClaire, Iowa, 1917*

Contents

Foreword	Michael Wolfe	
Scary Night at Napsinekee Hollow	Janet Willman	1
Rose and Edward's Tale of Love	Janet Willman	3
Letters to LeClaire	Connie (Corcoran) Wilson	7
The Legend of Tug Fest	Steven Lackey	27
Quit Claim Ghost	Debbie Smith	33
Mr. Boozy Just Came By	Rose Richardson	37
Smith Island by Compass	Darren Hall	41
A Grade "A" Ghost	Ron Leiby	65
Visitation	Heide Larson	77
Cold as the Grave	Theresa Davis	81
Ghost of a Life	Jannette LaRoche	97
The True Nature of Evil	Jannette LaRoche	111
Scourge of the River	Ellen Tsagaris	119

About the Editor

About Mary Eveline Parkhurst

About the Ghost Story Writers

Foreword

Michael Wolfe

I am an American picker and have been intrigued by the history of LeClaire since I was a kid.

As a young picker-in-training, I was intrigued by the old buildings and the historical objects found in them—so much so that I decided to hold on to them, share them, sell them. It was like holding on to the past and reminding us of what it was, what it meant. For me, each building was the site of a mystery just waiting to be told. From the stories of the Sac encampment to the growing village on the land given to Antoine LeClaire by those same natives, to the many tales of adventures along the Mississippi River, LeClaire is an ever-changing portrait of a river town that has evolved over the centuries.

To me, LeClaire's downtown is more than the set of restored and new buildings turned into eclectic shops and restaurants that it has become today. It is such a rich and historic river town inviting you to find the past and present through its people, its stories, and its growth from a hub for river pilots and railway stop to an interesting river attraction for locals and tourists alike. When heading east on Interstate 80, it is definitely worth the veer off of Exit 306 before heading across the river to Illinois. Like the stories presented here, LeClaire holds many surprises.

You know how much I like old stuff. I see the ghosts of LeClaire in every old building and shed. It is especially so on the levee where you can still hear the call of *Mark Twain* as if those pilots are navigating the river rapids, finding the depth where they won't hang up. So, I must tempt you to share in this glimpse of the past with me by reading these 13 ghostly tales that represent the images and faces of a LeClaire gone by, a past that meets the future, so we can better appreciate what it is today.

Mike Wolfe
Antique Archaeology
LeClaire, Iowa

Scary Night at Napsinekee Hollow

Janet Willman

It was a beautiful night for camping out and James had just gotten into the sleeping bag in the tent he was sharing with his fellow boy scout, Jake. This was the first time their scout troop had camped in Napsinekee Hollow and the scout leader had told stories around the fire of the Sauk Indians that had lived in the area, and how LeClaire's famous Buffalo Bill had been born in the hollow. Both boys were tired from all that day's events and they quickly fell asleep.

Suddenly James was awakened by a strange sound outside the tent. He looked over and Jake was still asleep in his sleeping bag so James decided to investigate on his own. Taking his trusty scout flashlight, he ventured out into the night. At first he thought the shadows around the fire were the scout leaders, but when he got closer to ask them if they heard the noise, he realized it wasn't his scout leaders at all.

Sitting on logs next to the fire were two warriors speaking in a language he could not understand. He was pretty sure they were Sauk because they were dressed just like the pictures he had seen when visiting Black Hawk Park in Rock Island. At first, James thought it was just a couple of the older scouts having fun, but looking closer he could tell they were definitely full-blooded Sauk. He didn't want them to see him so he quietly snuck back into his tent and hid deep in his sleeping bag.

When James woke up the next morning everything was back to normal, so he decided it must have just been a dream. A little later when he went by the fire, he found moccasin prints and a feather lying in the dirt.

Although he never could figure out an explanation for the strange evening, and although nothing bad had happened, he refused to camp out in Napsinekee Hollow ever again.

Rose and Edward's Tale of Love

Janet Willman

One cool foggy morning after moving to the Mississippi River town of LeClaire Iowa, I was walking along the riverfront and was overcome with a deep feeling of sadness.

As I turned and looked down the levee, I saw a young woman on the river's edge who appeared to be looking for something out over the water. She was dressed in a long skirt, hat and shawl that looked quite out of place for the current century. As I watched, she turned and saw a young man walking toward her along the shoreline. He was dressed in attire that reminded me of how my grandfather used to dress to go sailing. When the young woman saw him, she ran into his arms. As they embraced their images faded into the misty morning. Suddenly my sad feelings were replaced with a sense of comfort and joy. Confused and doubting what I had seen, I asked around town and learned the story of Rose and Edward's love.

In the late 1800s, Rose loved going to the levee on the Mississippi River with her papa and grandpa, the Baron, to meet the river boats that docked in LeClaire. Both men were riverboat captains who would pilot the steamboats through the treacherous Rock Island rapids between LeClaire and Davenport. Mama wouldn't allow Rose to go to the levee alone because of the roustabouts who hung out under the large rock elm down by the river.

Rose knew it was not the proper place for a sixteen-year-old young lady to be without the Baron or Papa accompanying her; yet, she would sneak down there every chance she got. Talking with and hearing stories from the river people who camped out under the large elm interested her. There was another reason Rose would go to the levee alone; she had met an eighteen-year-old deckhand named Edward and, after getting to know each other over the summer, they were sure they were in love.

Edward knew he could not ask Rose's papa for her hand in marriage until he had enough money to at least buy a decent ring. The winter weather was coming soon and Edward knew if he hadn't saved enough soon, he would have to move to a warmer climate to find work. That meant he wouldn't be able to see his sweetheart until the river ice thawed in the spring. That is why he was working extra shifts on any riverboat that would hire him.

Finally Edward was able to tell Rose that, after this one last job as a deckhand on the *Archer* towing barges to St. Louis, he would have earned enough to speak with her father. Rose had kept Edward a secret from her parents and she feared they would be disappointed in her for sneaking out and for planning to marry at such a young age. She decided not to risk having Papa turn Edward down, so she hid her packed bag and figured she would meet her love at the dock when the *Archer* was due to return. After writing a letter of explanation to her family, Rose snuck out and headed to the riverfront to await Edward the early misty morning the *Archer* was due in.

Arriving at the riverfront Rose saw that a crowd had gathered around the local constable. Constable Williams was telling the group that the *Archer* had collided with the *Die Vernon* five miles from the mouth of the Illinois River and that there were multiple casualties. Later that day, Rose learned from survivors that had returned to LeClaire that Edward had been one of the casualties from the terrible accident. It's said that no one could console the young woman, and, after several days of not eating or sleeping, she died of a broken heart wanting only to be with the love of her life, Edward.

I still walk along the riverfront and twice have witnessed Rose and Edward. It's comforting to know they eventually found each other and will be together forever.

Letters to LeClaire

Connie (Corcoran) Wilson

The envelope was postmarked August 1, 1923.

It bore a two-cent canceled stamp with George Washington's profile in the upper-right hand corner.

Return address?

Dr. Frederich Lamprecht, Physician and Surgeon,
411-412 Putnam Building,
Davenport, Iowa, Phone Dav. 610.

The heading: "Memorandum of Account: Statements Rendered Monthly." Dated July 1, 1923, the bill inside, which Jessie Cole had paid just before her death on August 10, 1923, was for $100.

One hundred dollars was a lot of money in 1923!

There was no further notation. Just, "Professional Services rendered to Miss Jessie Cole, LeClaire, Iowa."

"Of course, there wouldn't be any further details," thought her brother, Orvie. "The Doc would know enough not to put it in writing. Surprising he even sent a bill!"

As her only living relative, Orvie had been called back

from Regina, Saskatchewan, to bury his younger sister. Jessie was his only relative, as both their parents were now dead and there were no other surviving aunts or uncles. Orvie was heartbroken; "What happened, Jess? *What the hell happened?* Twenty-three! Twenty-three-year-olds aren't supposed to die! Who was it? WHAT was it?"

Orvie, standing by her coffin, looked down at his sister's pale face lying within the ornate oak casket, her dark hair cascading across the white cushioned pillow. The coffin was resting on a bier in the living room, positioned in the alcove on the south side of the North Cody house. Coal was delivered in a chute under that alcove, rattling down to the basement below.

"Good thing it's summertime. Otherwise, the coal would rattle down the chute, knock all the knickknacks in the window off, and disturb Jessie in her coffin on her final night on Earth," mused Orvie.

Orvie smiled at the memory of their childhood duties. It had always been Orvie's duty, as the older brother, to hurry home from school on coal delivery days and enlist Jessie's help in removing all the little glass baubles and trinkets that their mother liked to put on the window ledges. Otherwise, the glass items would be knocked from the window ledge when the coal rattled and rumbled in, and the glass pretties would break on the floor.

Not tonight, though.

Tonight was Monday, August 13, 1923, three days after Jessie's death, the night before her Tuesday morning funeral. "No fires tonight, unless you count the fires of hell," thought Orvie. But hell was not for his wonderful sister. Hell was for whomever sent her to an early grave.

This would be the last time Orvie would spend the evening with his sister. The last time he could talk to her, caress her cheek, ask her questions. Her beautiful brown eyes were closed. Her skin was smooth and pallid. Orvie reached out and touched Jessie's cheek. Cold. Beautiful, but cold as the grave.

The white dress she wore made Jess resemble a bride more than a corpse. But Jess had never been a bride.

Or a wife.

Or a mother.

Tears fell from Orvie's eyes. Rivulets ran down Orvie's cheeks, dampening his reddish-brown beard. He shook his head, ran his work-roughened hands over his face in a helpless weary gesture. He thought he heard Jessie's lilting melodic voice inside his head.

What was she saying?

Orvie's imagination was playing tricks on him. It

sounded like, "Keep looking, Silly."

Orvie didn't feel *silly*. He felt sad, mad and spooked.

Orvie's mind wandered, "He'd better hope I don't get my hands on him, if he knows what's good for him. Tomorrow, I will make an early morning house call on Dr. Lamprecht. Find out what he knows. $100 for 'services rendered'? This whole house only cost $40! What 'services' were you rendering, Doc? What did you do? And why? Who is responsible for this?"

Orvie paced the floor beside his sister's coffin, inconsolable, periodically glancing at Jessie's corpse reposing within the burnished oak casket.

Orvie was alone in the big old house on North Cody, just as Jessie had been alone in the big old house on the hill in LeClaire for nearly four months after their mother's death on March 31, 1923. For many months prior, Jess had been caring for Gertrude as she lay dying of what Jessie wrote to Orvie in Canada as "a leaky heart." (Orvie later saw the words "congestive heart failure" on their mother's death certificate.)

When Gertrude Cole died the last day of March, a Saturday, Jessie was plunged into deep grief. She had never considered her mother mortal. To Jess, Gertrude was a force to be reckoned with. Someone who would go on forever, but Gertrude had not gone on forever, and then Jessie was all alone with no one to comfort her, no one to talk to.

Had she been alone?

Orvie's fingers stroked his reddish-brown beard, pondering what he knew and what he didn't know. He definitely planned to find out everything there was to know about his sister's death.

When Gertrude died, Orvie had come down from the ranch in Regina for their mother's funeral. He had stayed one week. It was springtime and he needed to get back to planting the wheat and oat fields in Canada.

Aside from the grief both of Gertrude's children felt at the death of their last remaining parent, Orvie had not noticed anything amiss. In fact, he thought that Jessie looked good. Maybe she had gained a few pounds, but with her always-precarious health, that was desirable. She seemed sad, but she also radiated an indefinable inner glow. She was uncharacteristically silent during his time in LeClaire in the old family place, but he attributed that to the loss of their mother.

Orvie had asked her, "How are you holding up, Sis?"

"I will be all right, with God's help," Jess responded. "I've been lonely, of course, so I've been doing some reading and some writing."

"What have you written?" Orvie asked.

Jessie looked embarrassed, but she held out a tablet with a poem written in feathery Palmer script:

Of old your hand was on my head,
In happy days that long have sped.
Today, though we are worlds apart,
I feel it resting on my heart.

Orvie had looked at Jessie, who was obviously embarrassed at sharing her innermost thoughts. "That's lovely, Jess. I miss her, too. I wish I had been here before she passed. I should have been here." His brow furrowed.

Jessie said nothing, but wiped a tear from her eye with her embroidered handkerchief, JEC—Jessie Ellen Cole—on the lower right corner. She looked up at Orvie and finally said, "It's just something to keep me occupied, to keep me from thinking about how much I miss her, Orvie. I can't believe she's gone."

As Orvie began to examine the pile of correspondence and legal documents and bills and Christmas cards and old pictures that he had found in the family safe upstairs, he noticed one of his own letters to Jessie lay amongst the pile of documents in front of him.

Orvie examined his own letter to Jessie as though it were a letter from a stranger. The handwritten missive talked of how he had sold land in Canada for $50 more an acre than it had cost. He had made $10,000! There was one section where he advised Gertrude, their mother, not to worry so much about the $30 road tax. Another line from his own letter caught his eye, causing him to feel even more guilt: "The orchard and fruits are doing well. I had it named SunKist Farms, so when the corn crib is finished in the spring, I'll have a nice place for you and Mother to come join me in Saskatchewan. We have three seeders going all the time," wrote Orvie. "I shipped some horses up here to this town which is 260 miles from Regina." It had been spring when his mother had died.

Another story from one of Orvie's letters to Jess read: "Uncle John was in town last evening. He is going south next month to Indianapolis. Uncle John was telling Joe that the John Deere Plow Company has built a machine that will knock the one Joe was interested in patenting all to nothing. So much for all Joe's 'talk' and other people's money that he and Mr. James got people to invest in Joe's plow project. Joe has not got much to say now." That was the end of Joe's big talk about patenting a new plow that would put all others on the market to shame. And, soon, it was the end of Joe, himself, Uncle John's only child, and Orvie's cousin. Uncle John and Joe went totally silent after this November letter. Both had been killed in an automobile accident on their way to Indianapolis from Canada—the last of Gertrude's family gone.

Again, guilt struck Orvie.

"I should never have left Jess here alone to care for Mother. I should have brought them both to Canada. I should have written more often." Orvie thought of a portion of an old poem, "Of all the words of gods or men, the saddest are these: It might have been."

All he knew, for sure, was that he must find out what had happened to his sister, dead at such a young age. Yes, Jessie was often sickly, but the doctor had been vague on the phone about the cause of death, despite Orvie's persistent questions.

Atop the pile of letters and documents from the safe, which Orvie had now thrown on the coffee table in the parlor where Jessie, silent in death, kept her brother quiet company, was a Warranty Deed.

Orvie opened the 1872 deed of sale for the house from J. Wesley Rambo to James and Bridget Galliher. The house and lot had cost $40.

The deed was filed for record on November 26, 1872, at 10:30 o'clock, and recorded in Book 31 of "T" Lots on page 311. Then, of course, there was the inevitable mention of the house being "entered for taxation" as of November of 1872.

Nothing's certain but death and taxes, thought Orvie. *And lately there has been too much death in my life.* The Gallihers lived in the house on North Cody from 1872 until the entire Galliher family met death in a riverboat explosion.

The house was then sold to Orvie and Jessie's parents, James and Gertrude Cole. Gertrude and James Cole had moved into the house with two-year-old Orvie in 1900. That year, Jessie was born, a sweet, brown-eyed, brown-haired baby girl. The birth was hard on Gertie. After Jessie's arrival, the couple decided that their family was complete.

Jessie charmed everyone she met. However, her health was often precarious. A measles epidemic swept the area when Jessie was five. Her devoted mother nursed her back to health from the measles. Influenza nearly took Jessie at age eighteen in the flu epidemic of 1918, but, again, Gertrude cheated death by devotedly nursing her youngest child for weeks. Nearly a fourth of Jessie's classmates had died, but Jessie graduated from LeClaire High School, and became a music teacher, giving piano lessons in the parlor to the right of the house entry—the room opposite the one where she now lay. She was a longtime staunch member of the Presbyterian Church. Her best friend—(and, later,

Orvie's girlfriend)—was Nora Spinsby.

Orvie saw a list of other ladies of the parish who were assigned various duties. Jess, of course, was President of the Ladies' Aid Society, which met Thursday afternoons at two o'clock. The Secretary was Mrs. Richards. Sarah F. Miller was the Treasurer. Orvie scanned the scrawled pencil-written list to see if any of his high school classmates were among the members: "Membership Committee: Mrs. T. Wilson, Mrs. T. White, Miss Ida Holst, Mrs. Richards."

Nobody he knew there.

"Edith Richards was really getting a workout! Both committeewoman AND Secretary," thought Orvie.

Orvie continued reading the list: Mrs. W. Barnes, Hildy Comtt, Sadie Speer, Ida McFate, Helga Polleck, Neva Hulst. He scanned the "Flower Committee:" Susan Smith, Ella Hilaman, Mary McKnight, Joan Kirby, and Helen Weaver. Social Committee: Grace Wilson and Mabel Brown. Program Committee: Mrs. J. Tulis, Mrs. Wiserman, Mrs. T. Needam, and Mrs. C. Stewart.

The last name he saw was Nora Spinsby.

Seeing his old girlfriend, Nora's, name on the list gave him an idea. Nora and Jessie had been very close.

"I'll ask Nora what she knows. See if Dr. Lamprecht is a dead end." Orvie thought ruefully of the term *dead end.* Apropos. Nora had already been a tremendous help in arranging for the funeral service to be held tomorrow, August 14, 1923, Tuesday, at 10 o'clock at the First Presbyterian Church.

It was just now sinking in for Orvie Cole.

His 23-year-old sister was really dead. He had come from Canada not just to bury her, but also to find out what or who had killed her. Orvie was sitting here reading old correspondence he had written to Jessie over the past months, because he needed to be doing something in these last few hours before Jessie's body was buried, before the lovely girl he had known and loved as his younger sister and only sibling would go into the cold ground forever.

He couldn't simply go upstairs, turn off the light, and go to sleep. He needed to be near Jessie this last night. Her corpse rested not five feet away, awaiting burial on the morrow, the heavy casket, when brought into the room, gouged the floorboards forever, just as Jessie's loss would leave a lasting mark on Orvie's heart.

A crumpled bulletin from the First Presbyterian Church of Odebolt, Iowa, fell from the papers and drifted to the floor.

December 18, 1923.

The Reverend A.E. Adben, Pastor.

It caught Orvie's attention because it was of a different color and paper stock than anything else in the pile of old letters and documents. Then he noticed that it was from a church in a city nearly 300 miles away in Sac County, Iowa.

And then Orvie saw the letter in the envelope, tucked beneath the church flyer:

Dear Miss Cole:

I received your letter and was very glad to hear from you. Mrs. Adben went to Dubuque some weeks ago to the hospital where she underwent an operation. She is still there. I am afraid her condition is very serious at present. She is with her parents. I expect she will come home some months in the future, after she has recovered. Only God knows when.

The letter had been accompanied by a Christmas card, a small white cardboard postcard imprinted with a Santa's head above the message, "May Xmas find you happy and leave you happier still." Beneath this cheery message, there was a sketch of a fireplace mantel with stockings hanging from it. Handwritten was the message, "Dear Jessie, I am sending you this as a New Year's greeting, but wish, instead, it was a New Year's meeting. Happy New Year and many of them, Love, Adam."

The letter accompanying the card went on to discuss the growth of the Odebolt Sunday School; how it was a much easier task leading the parishioners of his new church in Odebolt, rather than the parishioners of the larger town of LeClaire. People in LeClaire had been surprised when the young pastor and his wife had announced they were leaving the picturesque riverboat town of LeClaire to move to Odebolt, nearly 300 miles away. Orvie thought he detected a note of rancor in the next paragraph of the letter to his sister.

"I do not hear from any one in LeClaire. I guess they have forgotten us or thought us not worth writing to. We hear very little aside from what you have written. I guess they think I did not treat my parishioners right. I hope and pray that you do not think that of me. I really appreciate your writing to me, Jessie. It means a lot to me. You were always special in the congregation and special to me. I hope you know this in your heart."

The letter continued, "I wish that I could step into your back door tonight. I am rather lonesome. I surely would enjoy a talk with you."

The rest of the letter went on to discuss the church

calendar. There was a saying framed in the bulletin:

We advertise ourselves and our church by what we do, not say, about it, as much as by what we do say.

This sounded contrived and confused and complicated to Orvie, who was a simple man of the soil. There was information concerning Easter, with a comment that Reverend Adben would travel to other Midwestern churches to help raise funds for foreign missions in the spring. Reverend A. (for Adam) E. Adben would be coming back to LeClaire in early April. Perhaps Reverend Adben would be able to see Miss Cole, if he made the trip?

Orvie put the letter down. The suggested return to LeClaire to raise mission funds would have taken place just after their mother died, in late spring. Jessie would have been at her most vulnerable. Old suspicions grew, flourishing in the darkness of night. Orvie finally drifted into sleep while still seated in the rocking chair near the casket. He didn't awaken until near dawn. He went upstairs to his old bedroom, threw off his clothes, and hoped he would be able to sleep before the sun rose in a few hours.

When Orvie had contacted Nora, his old high school girlfriend and Jessie's closest friend and confidante, and asked for her help in making arrangements for his sister's funeral because of the difficulty planning things when he was so far away in Saskatchewan, Nora had immediately volunteered, saying, "I'll be happy to help make arrangements, Orvie. I know just the minister Jessie would want to see her off to her eternal rest. He is a good speaker, and he knew Jessie well."

Then Nora said nothing.

At the time, Orvie had thought the silence represented sadness or grief. Perhaps Nora was angry with him for not contacting her previously on his own? Now, he was not so sure what to make of her silence. Orvie had worried no more about the necessary arrangements after contacting Nora Spinsby, other than to tell Nora that price was no object in selecting a coffin for his only sister.

"Buy her only the best," he instructed Nora.

Orvie knew that Nora would do a good job. She always did, at everything. He was not familiar with the local Presbyterian minister, since he had been gone from LeClaire for some time. It was a given that the First Presbyterian Church would hold the service, but the choice of an outside pastor had been Nora's.

It was only when Nora knocked on his door at eight in the morning to present him with the funeral program that Orvie realized that the minister at Jessie's funeral was to be none other than Reverend A.E. Adben, the married minister who had written the letters to Jessie that Orvie had sat up all night reading, sitting in the rocking chair in the parlor with Jessie's cold corpse lying nearby in the handsome oak casket. He spoke with Nora at length and learned many things.

The First Presbyterian Church at 10 o'clock was crowded with Jessie's friends and fellow members of the Ladies' Aid Society. It was a somber group.

The Reverend Adben stepped to the pulpit. He looked wan and drawn. Of course, he had to travel the 300 miles to reach LeClaire from Odebolt, near Storm Lake in Sac County, in time for the funeral.

He began, "Jessie Cole was President of the Ladies' Aid Society." After that bit of information, Adam appeared to clear his throat. He looked down at his knuckles. He bit his lip and continued. "Jessie was a loving sister (a glance at Orvie) and a caring daughter to her mother, Gertrude." Another pause. The pause lasted for a long time and the minister appeared to be fighting his emotions, holding back tears. He finally gathered his composure and continued, "God must have needed an angel in heaven, so he called Jessie home. Let us pray."

With that, the Reverend turned his back to the flock, but led the congregation in unison in reciting "The Twenty-third Psalm." His sermon had been very short, but the parishioners did not seem to mind or care. It was stifling in the small church, with no hint of a breeze. Adam clearly seemed stricken by Jessie's passing. It was unlikely that he could have continued speaking publicly without breaking down.

None of this was lost on Orvie. He watched his remarks with great interest. He also noticed that Adam was a handsome man, quite young, really, to already have been pastor of not just one but two churches. Orvie wondered why Adam had left LeClaire, a much larger and prettier town on the Mississippi River, to go to Odebolt in the interior of the state, a very small posting. Orvie was not the first to so wonder.

The interment ceremony in the family plot was very sad with several mourners sobbing openly. They were young friends of Jessie's. Young people do not accept death well as they are not used to death. Death is something that happens to other people, not to them.

After the burial, when the minister had thrown the clod of dirt on top of Jessie's coffin, intoning, "Dust to dust, ashes to ashes," Orvie resolved he would get the Reverend alone in the study of the family home to speak with him. Orvie had to sign some official documents regarding Jessie's death certificate. He asked the minister to join him, to assist him.

In truth, Orvie wanted something entirely different. When the two men were alone, Orvie was direct.

"What, exactly, was your relationship with my sister, Reverend Adben?"

The minister's composure dissolved immediately. He couldn't even pretend to be unaffected.

"I have sinned, Mr. Cole. I am a sinner. We are all sinners." The minister could not meet Orvie's steady gaze.

"What do you mean, sir?" Orvie's voice was rising.

"I do not think that Jessie would want us to dishonor her memory by discussing such things," replied Adam. "It is too late. What is done is done. It cannot be undone. She was an angel on Earth, and that is how we should both remember her."

"You visited her then, sir, in April, when she was alone and vulnerable. Am I to understand that this is the case?"

Again, Adam could not meet Orvie's gaze, which was enough confirmation for Orvie, who had met with Dr. Lamprecht earlier that morning and learned that Jessie's death had been caused by internal bleeding.

"Jessie was too far along," he told Orvie. "She told me different. I thought it would be safe."

Jessie bled out later, at home, alone and afraid to call for help.

At that moment, Orvie lurched forward across the desk in his study, blind with rage, intending to do great bodily harm to the Reverend Adben. As Orvie's hands closed on the Reverend's throat, a voice spoke softly.

It was unmistakably Jessie's voice. It was accompanied by a soft whooshing noise. The voice, clearly that of his dead sister, said, "Forgive him, Orvie, for he knew not what he had done."

Orvie was so shocked to hear his dead sister's voice, as clearly as though she stood before him, that he loosed his grasp on the minister's throat. Orvie fell back and collapsed into the desk chair in the study. The minister gasped for air and fell to the floor, landing on an area of wooden planking permanently gouged by the heavy casket.

Now, Orvie understood.

Jessie had never shared the knowledge of her situation with the father of her child or anyone else. She had tried to take care of the problem without letting anyone, including Orvie, know. This was so Jessie-like. She never wanted anybody else to worry about her.

Now, from beyond the grave, she had intervened to save the life of the man she had loved in life, the father of her child who did not even know of her condition until it was too late. Indeed, he might not know even now, unless Orvie were to tell him as he confronted him.

Ever since that fateful August day, a soft breeze often arises in the study of the house on North Cody. There is a whispering sound, a soft sibilance. The curtains rustle gently. The rocking chair in the room moves by itself. Many say they sometimes hear the sound of a woman softly crying in the upstairs bedroom, where Jessie's mother Gertrude breathed her last. The unmistakable sound of someone settling into the old rocker in the parlor, which can be quite unsettling when alone in the house, can be heard.

Orvie sold the house and returned to Canada, never to return. The house fell into disrepair. It was remodeled over the years, serving as everything from a family home to a candy-making enterprise before morphing into one of the city's eclectic shops.

But the majority of those who have been to the house on North Cody may still sense the presence of Jessie Cole and her unborn child.

The Legend of Tug Fest

Steven Lackey

The first time I heard this story was Halloween 2010. It started like this...

"The speaker spoke and while he read, I forgot all he said."

The speaker spoke and I could hear in my head, "Thump! Thump! Thump! " I could feel the electricity, taste the salt as sweat streamed down my face, see the carnival atmosphere, smell the aroma of hot dogs cooking, hear the band playing on this shore and the vague echo of the band on the other side of the river. My bones could tell something else echoed something powerful.

The story took me further back to the start of the contest long before the white man came to settle this area. For untold centuries, before anyone ever gave the names of Illinois or Iowa to the shores, natives joined in contest of strength. For hundreds of years, the spirits loved it. The warriors who lost were all pulled into the river, some drowned, and those who didn't were sacrificed until our ancestors stopped the slaughter. Without the blood to clean the spot, the spirits were able to take their power and bend the river here so it ran from east to west.

In the little town of Rapid City, Illinois, there is a plaque that tells of not how or why, but what took place 10,000 years where the river goes east to west in the greater Mississippi Valley.

The speaker spoke and told me of why the spirits scarred the land and the power expended would lay dormant for centuries—until—twenty four years ago, the Tug Fest started. The spirits watched and waited. Still, no one drowned no one was pulled into the river, or even into a pit of muck and mire.

It was civilized, sanitized, and so sterilized.

The spirits, without the sacrifices, felt quite starved for attention, unquenched. All that testosterone, the hormones, the adrenalin had to go somewhere.

The spirits grew angry.

They grew stronger!

As the speaker spoke, I knew why I made my yearly trek, first in the fall here at Buffalo Bill Cody Museum, here in LeClaire on Halloween, then, in the summer to Tug Fest.

Because the speaker spoke, some of us went to LeClaire, and others who had listened went to Port Bryon to watch the contestants. I watched their strongest, heaviest men take their spots on the tow line. Dozens of times that day the youngest and prettiest maidens flocked around their "warriors" like river gulls in a feeding frenzy. I watched in a panic-induced dread as the modern warriors picked up the steel cable, and dug their heels into the sand. I did not remember the story the speaker had implanted in my brain, what happened 10,000 years ago, and what to do if started to happen again...

I heard their chant of, "Pull that tow line! Pull that tow line!"

I felt the ground where the contestants stood grow hard, harder than 10,000 years before. I felt the cable grow stronger than any steel ever forged. I felt the people watching in Illinois and Iowa who heard what the speaker spoke and understood. I felt the agony of athletes who participated in this battle their arms and legs that screamed out in pain infused with energy not seen in the Quad-City area for 10,000 years.

Perhaps if it had been midnight instead of noon the contestants would glow like the spirits of the cosmos that fused them; we would have seen each body doing the tugging become infected possessed by the accent spirits.

"Pull that tow line!"

They pulled the tow line taught. They took up the slack. They made the red marker rise and dance above the muddy water.

Again the chant grew louder, "Pull that tow line!"

The single-minded effort to get that goal closer charged and recharged the spent arms and legs that pulled the cable till the marker did get closer.

"Pull that tow line!"

The closer it got the more they pulled.

"Pull that tow line!"

Inch by inch, the distance lessened.

They grew stronger.

"Pull that tow line!"

Their tunnel vision made the warriors see only the prize they sought almost within reach.

"Pull that tow line! Pull that tow line!"

Drowned all thought of self-preservation. The warriors did not feel the ground beneath their feet move. They did not see that the marker had not moved. It did not get closer to them.

They got closer to it. The shores started to move.

I saw the shores were closing. I knew if the spirits had their way the shores would shut and shift the river again. I was not alone. A collective gasp rose from those who heard this story last fall and countless falls before. I learned how to stop the chant of, "Pull that tow line. Pull that tow line! Pull that tow line!" At that point I remembered what the speaker spoke. I remembered what to do.

I, along with all of us who were dispatched from LeClaire last Halloween so we would come back here for Tug Fest each summer, yelled, "Drop that tow line! Drop that tow line! Drop that tow line!"

In an instant we all knew we were not there for a test of strength, of skill of sinew skin and muscle to compete, but to work together to defeat the spirits.

All warriors stopped. We had broken the spell. The Mississippi did not close.

The land snapped back before any damage occurred to the Quad-City valley. Dozens fell on their collective back sides never knowing why.

It only took five seconds for them to pick up the tow line and finish the match. A new spell of healing started no one knew what almost happened. No headline of earthquakes, no buildings falling like dominos—this time. The mighty Mississippi did not change again as it had 10,000 years ago.

All was safe—till next summer.

※

This year, I am the speaker and though you won't remember, some of you will go to Tug Fest again to hold off the spirits for another year. After hearing this tale, there are those of you who will go to Tug Fest to see the banks move again. Either way, invite a friend. When you go home tonight will you wonder if I implanted anything in your head?

Tonight I spoke, and while I read, you forgot all I had said.

Quit Claim Ghost

Debbie Smith

In 1975 we were looking for a house to buy. When the realtor showed us a new house being built in LeClaire, we were sold. I didn't know much about LeClaire but I did find out a little history. In February of 1834 the first house was built in LeClaire. The town was called Parkhurst back then. In 1855 Parkhurst, Middletown, and LeClaire were incorporated under the municipal governments as "Town of LeClaire". The house we purchased was on land that the Indians gave to Antoine LeClaire. We were now part of history!

After moving in we heard from the neighbors that there was an old run down two-story house on the site and they were glad it was torn down and a new one was built. They said the house was owned for many years by the O'Brian family. A neighbor boy said that Mrs. O'Brian had fallen down the stairs and died in the house. The house was on Jones Street. The abstract said that the O'Brian family kept quit claim deeding it back and forth in the family for a $1.00. It would go to one son then back to the parents. Then back to another son then back to the parents. Always for $1.00. I really wonder why!

We moved in September. By December, I heard the first story that lights were seen going on and off at night in the old house when there was no longer any electricity there. One neighbor said a ghost was seen in the backyard. They were assuming the ghost was Mrs. O'Brian. I thought this was funny. I didn't believe any of it.

My husband worked nights and we had a three- year old son and a three- month old daughter. Being in a new house and a new town I was a little scared and we all slept together in the bedroom that overlooked the backyard.

The first thing I noticed was an unusual amount of mist in the backyard. I knew there was a cistern buried out there and the mist seemed to always be over it. The dirt over the cistern always seemed to be sinking. We would put more dirt on it and it would sink again.

We had lived there about a week when we were awakened by a low echoing moaning sound. I looked outside to see if it was thunder or something but it was dark and a clear sky with a full moon. The kids woke up and started crying so by the time I got them back to sleep the noise had stopped. The next night I heard it again. My husband did not believe me and thought I was just homesick for our old house and old town.

Finally the weekend came and my husband was awakened hearing the same noise. He went outside and listened and thought the sound was coming from the cistern. The next morning, he began digging up the cistern. When he hit the top, he couldn't get it open.

He called the contractor who had built the house and he said the cistern was sealed with cement and there was no way he could open it as nothing could have been in there, and no pipes led to it to make any kind of noise.

The neighbors said the sound must be Mrs. O'Brian moaning. They said she was not found right away when she fell down the stairs. The house was built over the cistern and the stairs were above it.

Could this be her ghost moaning? I sure didn't know and I didn't want to find out.

We eventually put up an above ground swimming pool in the backyard and we never heard the moaning again. I like to think she is out there floating around in the water finally at peace.

Mr. Boozy Just Came By

Rose Richardson

I don't believe in ghosts!
I don't believe in ghosts!
I don't believe in ghosts!

That is what I kept telling myself; yet, how do I explain what happened at my house. We lived in LeClaire, Iowa, on Jones Street. Such a beautiful town with so much history. Our property was once even owned by Antoine LeClaire. Before him, Native Americans roamed on this land.

When my husband read the abstract to our home it talked of a man who had died in the house. When we sold the house several years later he once again looked at the abstract and the passage about the man dying was no longer there. He asked our lawyer if it was changed and the lawyer said, "No, that would be illegal." My husband was at a loss for words. How could that passage have disappeared?

Lots of things disappeared at that house. Every day I would miss something. I would tell the family that my good hairbrush was missing and no one had it. Then, in the morning, there the hairbrush would be in the middle of the living room floor.

One day, I looked everywhere for my rolling pin. I knew I had just washed it and left it in the sink to dry after I had made a pie. I asked everyone in the family and one visitor we had that day, but no one had seen it. Then, in the morning, there it was in the middle of the living room floor.

One day, I looked everywhere for my daughter's new shoes. They were so cute. Black with a little pink bow. They were nowhere to be found. By that time I just went to bed because I knew where to find them in the morning and I was right. When morning came there they were in the middle of the living room floor.

One night I was awakened by a scream from my son. I rushed into his room and he said over and over, "There is a ghost of a man in the living room!" We turned on all the lights, and of course searched everywhere, but no ghost was found. My Mom always said she had a ghost and named him Boozy, so we told the kids that Grandma's friendly ghost, Mr. Boozy, just came by to visit us. We did not want them to be afraid.

The ghost was never seen again, but the lost and found game continued for months. It was scary to think that it could possibly be someone getting into the house at night, but that was quite impossible with deadbolt-locked doors.

Yet, did our dead bolts work?

We would be watching television in the living room and we would hear the door open and close. We would go to see who came in and the door would be locked and no one was there. Then we would hear the doors upstairs open and close and we would look and no one was there.

A relative was having some health issues and came to live with us. The whole time he stayed with us, nothing turned up missing. I read somewhere that ghosts were actually afraid of people with certain problems.

Could that be true?

I really don't know, but we never again saw a ghost or had anything missing.

Smith Island by Compass

Darren Hall

On the whole river there was nothing that looked half so nautical. He resembled a pilot, which to a seaman is trustworthiness personified.
—Joseph Conrad, Heart of Darkness

The old man knew it was late to be fishing. Seventy years on the river had taught him that much. In September, the sun didn't sink into the horizon but rather dropped there like a stone. The wind had freshened, but he'd raised enough kids to know the ephemeral nature of a moment.

He'd sensed the fleeting nature of time even before his wife died, but that singular experience had solidified it. The Mississippi was by far the oldest friend he had left—and he had always offered it his respect. But a body of water, even one as magnificent as the Mississippi, doesn't offer the companionship of a living soul. And nearing eighty, his friendships had dissolved into formless spirits—with the exception of his great grandson.

"Papa, did you really used to jump off the railroad bridge when you were a kid?"

"Sure did. Did a lot of dumb things when I was a kid. Used to swim across the river. Wouldn't let you do that, though. Lot of things I wouldn't let you do that I did."

He watched the boy squint, trying to imagine his great-grandpa jumping off the I74 Bridge stretching across the river in the distance. He started to tell him that the bridge he'd leapt off was down river a fair piece. Started to tell him that bridge, like a lot of things, had disappeared decades before the boy was even born. But he saw the child's mouth hang open, and decided against it. Instead, he reached out and tugged the boy's life jacket, then turned into the auxiliary canal that would eventually take them into Green Gables harbor, LeClaire. He'd taught him much about the river, and he could see the boy becoming one with the waters. Yet there was so much more to learn, and time had become an enemy.

"Probably be the last boat through here this fall," the young guy at the top of the lock yelled. For an instant the old man sensed the operator above him was in a similar frame of mind. Then he saw the man rest a foot on the rail above them, bow his head, and start toying with his phone.

No, he wasn't seeing the same expanse of river, he thought. He's marking the time.

The old man nodded to the man's indifferent frame and tried once more to quit thinking about the past. Seemed like yesterdays and lasts were about all he thought about these days.

"What's he mean, Papa, about us being the last boat through here?"

"It's Sunday night. Not many people still on the river. They usually close on Labor Day weekend—it's open a couple extra weeks this year 'cause people like us are trying to soak up the last warmth before winter."

The kid nodded, then turned to watch the lock in front of them open slowly.

To the kid, the process was intriguing. Sure he chattered a lot, but the old man could tell he was a watcher, too. Like now.

Holding the tip of his pole six feet above the edge of the water, the boy was soon busy marking the water's rise in the locks.

The man on the rail above him was still toying with his phone.

"Be careful," the young man at the lock eventually mumbled. "Looks like there's a storm heading this direction.

Water can get pretty rough in a hurry."

The old man cranked the engine on the flat-bottomed boat and started to say something clever. *My great-grandfather was piloting boats down this river 150 years before you were born, or I've forgotten more about this river than you'll ever learn.* But he simply nodded, offered a half-hearted salute, and motored slowly down the length of the lock.

"You didn't unbuckle those straps again, did you?"

"No Papa."

The old man had felt foolish when he'd dropped the life jacket on the conveyer at Wal-Mart. Kind of thing his wife would've done. But the kid loved it—crazy cartoon character stretched across it wasn't even an animal, looked more like the kind of sponge he'd use to clean the sink. The old man reminded himself to check the snaps again when they anchored— pull needlessly on the bands as if he the mere act of caution could protect the boy from the future stretched out in front of him.

"How come you don't have names for any of the rocks and stuff along here?"

"What do you mean, names for the rocks?"

"I don't know. Seems like every time we're out fishin' everything looks the same to me and then you'll say, 'That's Campbell's Island where Blackhawk attacked so and so."

This is why he took the kid fishing, he thought. Other people treated him like an obstacle in their way—they rushed past with barely a notice. But the kid? The kid listened to him.

"Here, hand me your pole. Cast it toward the bank," he said, then the old man cast the line deep into the still water of the canal along Smith Island one more time.

"Papa, tell me again where the ships used to wreck?"

The old man's fingers fought the tiny line, wound it once more through the eye of a lure, and pulled it tight with his teeth.

"Ships went down all along this river. This little canal wasn't a part of that. This was made so fishermen like us don't have to go through those big locks over there."

"So no ships wrecked back here?"

"Not that I know of. Most of the steamers crashed a few miles downstream— closer to where you live in Rock Island. I don't know exactly where every ship crashed, but the reason LeClaire exists is because of this little stretch of water."

"What do you mean?"

"I mean the waters between here and your house were shallow rapids a hundred years ago. They'd hire men like your great, great, great grandpa to pilot the boats through the rough water. If they tried to do it alone a lot of them didn't make it."

"So people died?"

The old man stopped mid-cast, lowered the pole and looked squarely at the boy.

"Yes. They died son. It's been happening since the beginning of time. It's nothing to be afraid of, though."

He watched the kid's eyes trace the thick trees along Smith Island, before studying the dark bank of clouds building in the west.

"So are there still bodies in this river?"

The old man flipped the lure across the front of the boat and smiled. "Bodies? No." He paused. "I don't know. Maybe. But there's nothing to be afraid of."

"Have you ever seen a ghost, Papa?"

"A ghost?" He flipped the pole down to his hip and sent another long cast toward the bank. "No. Seen some strange things, though. Mighty strange."

"What do you mean strange things?"

"Oh, I'm an old man. Get to be my age; you've seen all

kinds of things.

"Like what?" the boy asked, fidgeting with his ball cap.

The old man reeled in his line, working it away from the edge of the boat, and tied the treble hook to the eyelet.

"I don't know. Was down river a ways one night. This was a long time ago, back before I had the sense I do now. I was with your grandma—hadn't known her very long, and it started getting a little foggy. She started saying, 'Hadn't we better get back to LeClaire.'

The kid flipped his pole toward the bank, but the line wrapped around the end of it and instantly a long spool of fishing line emerged in the bail like a bird's nest.

The kid sighed, handed it to his great-grandfather.

"You don't understand now, Tiger, but someday you're going to do stupid things just because you want a woman to think you're brave." He wanted to add, and *I won't be around to save you*, but stopped short. Didn't want to be one of those old men always talking about his death. Instead, he simply said, "I'd gotten to braggin' about how my family had been movin' up and down this river for a hundred years. Told her I could navigate this stretch of river with my eyes closed."

The old man worked the line taught and tossed the kid's line into the river.

"Could you? Could you get back and forth with your eyes closed?"

He laughed. "No, we started heading down the river that night, and I swear that fog moved across this river like someone had dropped a blanket on it. You know what courage is, Son?"

The kid shook his head.

"Courage is being scared, but you're the only one who knows it. I got real scared that night. Real scared. Doesn't take long on the water before everything around you looks exactly the same."

"Is that why you carry that thing?"

The old man touched the compass tucked in his shirt pocket, thought about his wife—remembered how she'd bought it for him that first Christmas they'd been married.

***

He'd married young, wanted to be old at 20, experience in the ways of life. Having neither fought in WWII, like his brother, nor captained steamships, like his father, he wondered whether he was accomplishing anything. He certainly wasn't about to resign himself to a laboring job at the newly opened ALCOA plant. Not for long, anyway. He *was going to make his mark on the world.*

They'd been married less than six months when she'd told him—pregnant. One simple word and he'd reacted like a fool, left for the bar and didn't come home until most of the wages he'd earned that week were gone. The light he'd seen in her eyes had cast a shadow across his future—no traveling the world, no striking out in quests for adventure and squandering fortunes.

And he'd been right, too, but only in the outline of the future, not in the details. Sixty years later he still carried that compass. But not as a reminder of that night he'd almost lost them on the river, and not as a reminder of his wife. He carried the compass to always remember gratitude, and to acknowledge that sacrifice, love, and the present are the most important ingredients for happiness.

He hadn't understood that then, thought silence and anger were the most certain way for a woman to understand his position.

"*Why in the world are you spending this kind of money on something like this? For God's sake, Dorothy. We can barely pay the rent. You're taking it back tomorrow,*" *he'd finally barked.*

"*I can't,*" *she'd screamed, but the thick wood door of the bathroom had muffled the remainder of her words.*

"I'm not a river man! I'm working on an assembly line! What in the world am I going to do with an expensive compass on the river, anyway?" he'd spat.

"Cling to it," he mumbled, feeling the weight of the memory in his hand.

"What'd you say, Papa?"

"Nothing," he said, and tucked the compass back in his shirt pocket.

"Papa, can I hold your compass?"

"Of course you can. Of course."

"So what happened that night on the river? You never told me. Did you get lost?"

"What happened," he repeated, still uncertain himself.

Seventy-nine years old and he'd never told anyone about that night. Not another living soul. Not even his wife, not all of it anyway.

"I'd always assumed it was one of the men from the Fannie Harris," he finally began.

"What men?'

"It was a wreck. One of many along this stretch. I used to see some strange things down there. I don't know. Even when I'm by myself on the river, I've never felt alone, you know?"

"I talk to my stuffed animals," the boy said, and the old man nodded in understanding.

"There was a couple of fireman who went down with that steamer."

"Firemen?"

"Not that kind of fireman. Old ships had special firemen that kept it running."

"Did you ever see, like, a ghost?"

"No, nothing like that. It was just a weird feeling. Hard to explain."

The boy studied him, nodded, and retraced the river with his eyes. "Grandpa, I think we better get home."

The old man circled the lure along the edge of the boat, brought it up, and carefully tied it to the eye of the pole. He looked into the wide eyes of his great grandson, watched him fiddle with the compass—wrapping the chain around his finger and dropping the compass until it snapped tight and bounced. The old man took one last look down the river; saw the deep orange of the sunset soaking into the horizon behind him, and the dark clouds building beneath them, tried to snap a mental picture of the moment for the long, lonely winter in front of him.

"What happened, Papa," the kid finally whispered.

"I saw a light in front of me. Not a bright light, but a light. I just kept following it—real slow like. Kept thinking in the fog it might be close or it might be real far off. Didn't know what kind of ship it was, but figured if I stayed close, eventually I could follow it right into lock 14 over there."

"What was it?"

"Don't know. Crept behind it for almost an hour, and when I finally got close enough to the locks to see what it was there wasn't anything in front of me. Not a darned thing."

"So, it was like a ghost?"

The old man just shook his head.

"Don't know what it was. My grandpa taught me a long time ago not to panic. Take a deep breath and keep movin' forward. He also taught me that there are things on this river—things that don't always make sense. But you can't panic. You have to trust the spirits of the river."

The old man saw the boy shiver and knew it wasn't from the cold.

"So there are ghosts out here?"

"I don't know. I just know a lot of people lived and died along these banks—remember those old ruins on Smith Island? People, Indians included, been living here a lot longer than we have."

"I'm not afraid of ghosts, Papa."

"I know you're not, Son."

The old man tucked the pole along the inside of the boat and turned to the motor.

"We'd better get in, though. I am a little afraid of your mother."

Papa soared over the impressive houses lining the riverfront—visions of riverboat men at once ephemeral and tangible as they worked their cargo up and down the water. Time itself was both linear and exponential now. He didn't know where this vision would take him; he merely knew, by now, the trip would be beyond his control.

Then he saw the boat, his boat, alone in the middle of the canal. The sunset, no longer a warm promise of extended fall, but rather, a forgotten orange wink disappearing behind a thick bank of winter clouds.

He knew for certain he was almost home, but he fought the urge to move beyond the river into the beckoning beyond.

The child's pull still too strong.

Children still believed in magic, didn't question

wonders, but rather, embraced them as a reality. And enchantment was all the old man's spirit had left.

Strange the way knowledge alters a landscape. Experience allows us to see, Papa thought. Yet it taints our vision of all that surrounds us. The empty boat— a child's life jacket flopped on the rear seat—and for the last time on this earth his response had been emotional: panic.

Maybe it was the heave the boy made pulling up the anchor. Maybe the child had leaned over the edge—trying to study a gray shadow beneath the water. Regardless, the boy Papa had been watching, albeit it seemingly more and more each day from a distance had tumbled, splashless, and gone.

How many years had it been since he'd dove into the icy water? How long since he'd floated on a horizon as endless as a spool of fishing line? Something happened in that moment, though. The old man didn't see his life flash before his eyes, not the marriage and five children or the dozens of grand and great-grandkids scattered throughout the country. No. He'd already replayed those films a thousand times. Instead, Papa saw nothing but black and empty space, and the hollow seat at the back of the boat. He took a deep breath— a full, long, calming inhale. His years had shed like the crimson leaves of a tattered oak.

He willed the life jacket into the water and dove headlong into the water, fearless and calm.

He didn't notice the cold. Didn't feel the weight of his heavy boots or the thick flannel shirt tight against his chest that he always seemed to be fiddling with on his nightly journeys down the river. His eyes were open, searching with a clarity he knew he no longer possessed.

The seconds built a tower of pain in his chest, and he cleared the surface of the water with a heavy gasp. Greedy for oxygen, his hands splashing through the haze and landing without force in the water.

He looked left. Right. The boat merely mocked him—spinning and rocking gently in the distance. He took a gulp of air. He dove. Resurfacing, the loud click of a stopwatch seemed to echo in his ears, but strangely the ticking was merely a calming reminder of the endless nature of time.

He dove again.

This time, when he resurfaced, he saw something. No more than five feet from him. Hovering above the haze: a simple, shimmering glow.

He didn't question the significance. Didn't ponder the line separating faith from skepticism, or the hollow darkness that had filled him for the final months of his life.

Instead, he dove toward it.

In eighty years, he'd known joys and sorrows, anxiety and triumph, even the absolute terror of desperation. What he'd never known on earth, not fully anyway, was the absolute certainty of peace.

As he watched the clutching grasp of a tiny hand clinging frantically to the life preserver, he finally knew tranquility.

"Hold me, Papa!" the boy gasped.

The old man tried to whisper in his ear, tried to tell him that he'd never let him go. Never. But the words were lost in tears as the boy kicked toward the boat.

Papa tried to shove him, but the boy shimmied up the side of the craft without his help. Papa looked around the whole expanse of river—taking it all in for one eternal moment. He took one last look around, sensing the presence around him, and his eyes locked on the glowing shape twenty feet from the boat.

"Lay flat on the bottom," he said, but the words were swallowed by the wind.

The old man craned his neck one last time in the darkening night.

"Thank you, Papa," the boy stuttered. "I'm so sorry Papa. I love you."

The old man floated along the side of the boat, and for

the first time he started to feel the cold, not uncomfortable, but creeping into his soul with a steady pulse.

"Put your life jacket back on, Bud," he mumbled, and then floated to the back of the boat.

There was nothing but the lapping of water against the side of the vessel—the sky in the distance now a black wall of darkness. He could hear the chattering teeth of his grandson, feel the waves begin to build around him.

"Can I make it home, Papa?" The kid paused, the wind making his voice sound small even in the short distance between them.

"I'm not scared, you know," he finally whispered.

"You're coursing river blood," the old man said, reaching a big hand inside the boat and trying to toss an old coat toward him. The kid rolled over and grabbed it on his own. Papa watched him wrap the long coat around his small body, his whole form disappearing beneath it. "We've never lost any cargo on this river, and we ain't about to start now," Papa whispered, the words one final reminder of the linear timeline of existence.

"Papa?" the boy whispered.

"I have to go, son. You're getting older now, you know? You have to learn to respect the river. It's a wonderful place, but no one makes it up and down this river by himself.

Remember that, okay boy?"

"Papa."

The old man looked at the light in the distance, the glow become less a shimmering ghost, than, crystallizing figures—his wife, his father, a grandfather, the son they'd lost too soon...

"I need you Papa."

"I have to go, boy. You'll make it. I'll always be here, son. Always."

The old man could sense calmness in the boy, an innate and rational understanding encompassing both the past and the future.

⁓

The child watched a hazy shadow slip past the boat, and he instinctively drew his gaze downward to the shiny compass he'd been clutching in the darkness. For the first time in a month, the boy finally understood what his Papa had meant.

His Papa was gone and courage must be found alone.

"I'm out here," the boy yelled in the darkness, but his voice felt pitiful and small—and the wind was now heavy in his ears.

He considered his Papa's words again.

"I'm coming in," he shouted, his tone gaining confidence and strength.

It was early November, and his Papa was gone—had been gone for nearly a month now. Wouldn't be back, not in the way he wanted him, anyway. The boy understood that now. Understood what his mother had told him nearly every day for a month. Understood what the lady at school had been trying to tell him in her tiny office smelling of sweat, desperation, and lilacs.

Deep down he'd known for a while. When he'd worked tirelessly to unhitch the boat from the cleat—terms like half hitch and bowline were swimming somewhere in his mind, not quiet close enough to grasp.

He'd felt it when he'd shoved from the dock an hour ago and let the current slowly drift him into the channel.

For the first time in nearly a month he hadn't felt alone.

Now he could see the glow of the emergency vehicles gathering from Green Gables all the way to the auxiliary lock. Could hear the muffled voices of men barking orders, and the distinct, shrill scream of his mother. And for the first time tonight he wanted to go home.

"I'm out here, Mom," he yelled, but his voice was losing strength. This time it was merely a whisper: "Come get me, Mom," he sobbed softly.

He wanted to try the sputtering motor again, but thought better of it. One trip into the water tonight had taught him enough. He slipped the old coat from over his shoulders, and with shaking fingers worked the life jacket around his shoulders and fastened it around his small chest.

In an instant the river seemed to fill with light—voices and boats surrounding him, the channel shrinking into little more than a stream.

"Oh honey," his mom cried. "Oh honey. We were so scared. So scared."

"I'm okay, Mom," he tried to assure her, and for once, he meant it.

"So worried," he heard her say again.

"Papa had to go," he said in explanation.

An instant later he was hoisted across the bow of the boat and was swallowed in his mother's arms.

"Don't you ever do this again," she sobbed.

"I'm fine, Mom. Really. Papa had to go."

"Oh, baby. He's gone, buddy. He's gone," she wept, but didn't seem to recognize that he understood.

"I know, Mom. I know that now."

That stopped her. For the first time she seemed to actually take him into her gaze.

"You know that?"

"I know Mom. He was here; he helped me out of the water. He went to be with Grandma, Mom. He's gone."

A stranger wrapped a blanked around him.

"I took the boat from the marina. Papa said I was a captain. Said I had it in my blood. I'm not ready, Mom. I lost control of the boat. I tried to start the motor."

He tried to say it all in one breath—fell in, I was so scared under the water. I couldn't breathe.

He saved me.

He was here.

Instead, he simply clung to his mother and wept.

"Honey you're soaked," she said, still unaware of what he'd seen.

"I know. I fell in the river. Papa pulled me out of the water and helped me back into the boat. He's gone, Mom. I know that now."

This time her tears didn't pour. This time she recognized the boy she thought she'd lost.

"You do know, don't you?"

"I know. He said goodbye, Mom. I held his compass," he said, offering the last piece of assurance she would need. But it didn't hit its mark. In fact, it seemed to completely deflate her.

"Honey, we buried that with your Papa. I tucked it under his suit jacket myself before we closed the casket."

A wave of sadness seemed to swallow her.

The floor of the boat shifted beneath them as a large, bearded man moved from the fishing boat and boarded the rescue vessel.

"Guys, we better get these boats to shore. It's probably just a small storm, but it looks like the kid is pretty wet already."

"Thank you, Jim. Thank everyone for us," his mother whispered.

"Everyone's just glad he's safe," the man said, taking one large step back down into the fishing boat.

The burly man started to squat in front of the motor, but instead reached down and grabbed something from on top of the seat.

The boy and his mother watched him from the other boat, but even in the darkness they both knew what he was holding. He moved to the edge of the boat, steadied himself by grabbing the railing of the nearby craft, and dangled the length of chain and compass in front of the boy.

"You might be needing this, son. A captain can't be without his compass."

A giant flash of lightening lit up the night, and the boy

turned the object and stared at the inscription engraved on the back.

Cliff,
May the river always lead you back to me.
Love,
Dorothy

A Grade "A" Ghost

Ron Leiby

It was a bright and beautiful summer day. The weather was superb. The flowers, especially the Hollyhocks that started blooming in early June, were out in full color all over LeClaire. The year was 1952. For Lucy Maye Stewart it was soon to be the beginning of a bright new life and career.

She had graduated from the Albert Gross School in May. Mrs. Rodgers, who was one of her closest and favorite teachers, had convinced a local businessman to offer her a job in the Fall as an accounting clerk. Although she was excited about her prospects and was looking forward to starting her new job, she was also looking forward to a summer of fun. After all, she had worked very hard during her last year of school. As a result of Mrs. Rodgers' tutoring, she was able to earn straight A's in all of her subjects. In addition to being recognized by her teachers as an exceptional student, she was also very helpful, eager to be of assistance to each of them whenever the need arose.

In fact, they all agreed she was an all around grade "A" student. Lucy Maye figured she deserved a few months off. It was time to relax and she fully intended to enjoy the summer months with her friends and family.

But first, she had one last item to take care of. Along with some of her classmates, she had volunteered to help the teachers clean out their desks and pack away books and other school materials. It was kind of a tradition for each year's graduating class. It wouldn't take long, and if they started early in the morning, they would be done by noon.

It was not to be. Lucy Maye was destined to be locked in that school forever. Her volunteer work there would never end. She would never start her new job, never get married and raise a family, and never, ever, enjoy a beautiful, bright summer day of fun again.

Lucy Maye and some of her other classmates arrived at the school at eight in the morning to find the teachers already there. Mrs. Rodgers had volunteered to be in charge. In operation since 1926 and, until its closure in 1966, the school included grade levels of one through twelve. There were two floors with the principal's office at the top of the stairs. The school also had a lower level. The student volunteers were assigned various tasks and were determined to finish all of them as soon as possible.

Everyone was scurrying about on each floor, carefully packing books and other educational supplies into boxes, and then placing them on shelves in the basement storeroom. Several times the teachers instructed them to slow down, especially while carrying the boxes down the stairs. They assured them the job would not take long and they would soon be out enjoying the rest of the day.

Several hours later, with almost all the books and materials packed and stored, most of the students gathered by the front doors. A handful them, including Lucy Maye, helped the teachers clean out their desks and then boxed and stored the few remaining items. After the last tasks were complete, the teachers gathered all of the students together and thanked them for their help. All worn out, the students were glad the job was done, and eager to leave. As the teachers and students exited the front door, no one seemed to notice that Lucy Maye was not among them. Watching what she believed to be the last of the students walk away, Mrs. Rodgers locked the front door, got into her car, and left.

Later that afternoon, Lucy Maye's mother was concerned about her daughter's whereabouts. She had told her mother she would most likely be home by lunch or soon after, but it was now almost four o'clock and there was no sign of her. Her mother contacted one of the teachers and was told that everyone had left the school at about 11:30 that morning.

Now she was very concerned. Her daughter would have come home for lunch before going somewhere with her friends. After talking with a few of Lucy Maye's friends and finding they hadn't seen her since they left the school, she was now getting frantic. She contacted Mrs. Rodgers, who was the teacher in charge of the cleanup, and asked about Lucy Maye's whereabouts. Mrs. Rodgers was now concerned too. She started to think that perhaps she had locked Lucy Maye in the school by mistake. They both decided to go to the school.

What Mrs. Rodgers and everyone else did not know was that Lucy Maye, while carrying the last box down the stairs, had lost her footing and fell down, dropping the box of supplies and slamming her head against one of the steps as she tumbled to the bottom. She had then stood up, staggered about in a daze for a second or two, and then collapsed onto the lower hallway floor, adjacent to the stairs, just out of sight. Her lifeless body lay there on the floor while the others were helping the teachers carry their personal belongings out the front door. With all the students in a hurry to leave, a hasty and erroneous count had been made by Mrs. Rodgers. Satisfied the count was correct, she had thanked the students and bid them goodbye and good luck..

Upon arriving at the school, Lucy Maye's mother and Mrs. Rodgers didn't notice anyone looking out any of the front windows. They quickly opened the front door and entered the school.

Immediately they both started shouting Lucy Maye's name. There was no answer. They checked the rooms on each of the floors and found no one. About to leave, Mrs. Rodgers decided to check the store room in the basement. When she reached the bottom of the stairs, she was startled to see Lucy Maye lying off to one side of the hallway, her head in a pool of blood. After recovering from the initial shock, she went to Lucy, crouched down and turned her over, trying to get a response, but to no avail.

Just as she was checking for a pulse, her mother came down the stairs and seeing Lucy, started screaming. Mrs. Rodgers tried to calm her down. Leaving Lucy Maye's mother holding her daughter, she went up to the Principal's office to see if the telephone was still working. Thankfully, it was. She had the operator call the town constable. Along the way, he picked up the local doctor. Upon arrival, the doctor examined the body and pronounced Lucy Maye dead. Her body was removed and taken to the local funeral parlor. Later, the Scott County authorities ruled the death a tragic accident.

It was overcast with very dark clouds the day Lucy Maye's funeral services were held. It rained off and on all day. In addition to her fellow classmates, many of the local teachers, including Mrs. Rodgers, and half the town, attended her funeral. Although the splendid display of flowers at the funeral seemed to brighten up the parlor, it was still a very sad affair for everyone. For many of Lucy Maye's friends, the fun filled summer they had previously looked forward to, never happened. They, along with many other towns people, were glad to finally see the fall season begin.

Fall meant that school would be in session and students would have their minds on their studies, instead of the loss of a dear friend. As for Lucy Maye's fellow classmates, some went on to college and others started careers of their own. Most just went on with their lives. Hopefully, within a year or so, Lucy Maye's death would just be a sad memory, one they would just as soon put out of their minds forever.

However, almost immediately, strange things started happening after the new school year began.

They were just little things here and there that were noticed, mainly by the teachers, especially Mrs. Rodgers. One day, before classes began, Mrs. Rodgers spilled a cup of coffee on her desk and went to get something to clean it up. Arriving back at her room, she was puzzled to find the spill was already taken care of. No one admitted to doing it. Another day, she was finding it hard to hear the students in her class because of some noise in the hallway. As she walked toward the open hallway door to close it, the door suddenly closed, seemingly by itself. Even her students were puzzled by what they saw that day.

In addition to these strange happenings, after school had let out one afternoon, she had stumbled in the hallway, dropping her grade book and some student papers. After recovering, she picked up the items and took them to her classroom. Noticing that her new pen was missing from the grade book, she figured it must still be out in the hallway and went back to get it. Not finding the pen anywhere, she returned to the classroom and discovered to her amazement, that it was right on her desk, in plain sight.

A couple of times when Mrs. Rodgers was in her classroom by herself, grading papers, she thought she heard someone say her name, only to look up and find no one else in the room. Teachers began to talk to each other about these things, along with the countless other experiences that baffled them and some of their students. They could never come up with any obvious answers.

Over the years, everyone, including students and teachers, started to attribute these events to Lucy Maye. They figured Lucy Maye's spirit was roaming throughout the school, still helping the teachers as she had been doing before she died. One might try to attribute any or all of the "little things" that happened over the many years to follow, just coincidences, if it were not for the one thing that seemed to pull them all together.

Almost every year since Lucy Maye's death, about the time the graduating seniors gathered to help the teachers clean up, they would hear strange noises coming from within the school. After the doors were locked and they all began to leave, the front doors would start to rattle, as if someone was still in the school, trying to get the doors to open. The teacher in charge would always walk back up to the entrance doors, unlock them and look inside, halfway expecting to find a student had been accidently locked in. But no one was ever there. Some years the doors would not rattle, but then some of the students would swear they could hear banging on some of the school windows.

Then, the holy grail of all unexplainable things

happened. One year, as the graduating senior class was helping the teachers clean out their rooms, Mrs. Rodgers knew she would not be back. It was to be her last year at the school. After thirty years of teaching, she was finally retiring. Although she knew it was the right time for her to go, she was still a little sad about it. She would miss this school and all of her students. At the end of the day, with everything cleaned and stored for the next year, all began to leave. Mrs. Rodgers would be the last one out the doors.

After she had accounted for all the students and teachers, she locked the doors, and started for her car. The volunteer students were many paces ahead, with their backs to her, and the other teachers were getting into their cars. Suddenly, out of the corner of her eye, Mrs. Rodgers thought she saw movement in one of the windows and quickly turned to look back at the school. Freezing in her tracks, she was a little surprised to see one of the students looking out of a second story window from inside the school, smiling and waving at her. She was absolutely sure everyone had been accounted for. Who could it be? As she started back up the stairs to the door, she stopped for a moment and looked back up at the girl in the window.

Although she could not believe her eyes, deep within her heart, she knew who it had to be. Taking a deep breath and gathering up all of her strength, she smiled and waved back. She saw the girl smile again, and then slowly fade away.

She would later swear the girl looked just like Lucy Maye. She was even wearing a red dress, the same color dress Mrs. Rodgers had remembered her wearing, many years ago, on the last day she had seen her alive. She thought about catching up with the others and sharing her experience with them, but then thought it was best not to. She figured this was between her and Lucy Maye. Mrs. Rodgers thought to herself that somehow Lucy Maye knew she would not be back and she came to say goodbye. She walked slowly to her car and opened the door. Taking one last look back at the school, and seeing nothing, she got in and drove away, never to return.

The old "Albert Gross" school building, which is still standing, hasn't been used as a school since 1965. Two new Grade schools; Bridgeview and Cody, were built in 1966 to handle Kindergarten through sixth grades. Pleasant Valley Junior High School serves seventh grade through eighth, and Pleasant Valley High School serves students in the

Sophomore through the Senior class. The old Albert Gross building, owned by the City of LeClaire, is now leased by the Community Improvement Corporation of LeClaire, a non-profit organization. Although none of its members have ever experienced anything out of the ordinary over the years (at least nothing they will admit), it has been noticed that when passing the school, especially in the early evenings, just before darkness begins to fall, strange noises can be heard coming from the building.

Lucy Maye's helpful and lonely spirit must be drifting from floor to floor, classroom to classroom, trapped for eternity in her former school. Poor Lucy Maye has become a grade "A" ghost with nothing to do, nowhere to go, and no teachers to help. Perhaps, sometime in the future, Mrs. Rodgers's spirit will come back for Lucy Maye and lead her into the light of a bright and beautiful summer day.

Visitation

Heide Larson

It had been almost a half century since I'd seen Anna.

I went to my childhood friend's memorial with the instinct that past friends matter. It was a pathetic little affair, the sister of the departed having thrown it together several months after Anna's parting, hosting it out in the middle of nowhere Iowa. She had personally invited 50 and put it in the newspaper five days prior to the gathering. I'd read the announcement in my hometown newspaper online. It looked to me only about ten people showed up on the windy fall day to the cabin rented out for happy or sad commemorations, in a wooded area just outside Iowa City. The drive from LeClaire seemed short, as if my car had entered a magnetic field within which it was being pulled to its destination.

Theresa was surprised to see me, as we'd drifted from childhood into our own adult orbits many years and miles apart. It had once been a large family, diminished by car accident (the eldest), by failed surgery (the father) and by natural cause (the mother). Anna had been the sibling my age, Theresa her older sister.

When it came my turn to reflect on a life remembered, I spoke of what little I could recall of my once very close friendship: playing Barbie dolls next to the ivy covered wall facing the side of her house; enviously combing her long black hair smooth as liquid gold; sitting in the back seat of her father's car when he drove us to school and cowering under his tyrannical persona, yet feeling safe with Anna by my side. I ended these exhumed memories with a poem by Emily Dickinson. Others followed with their personal experiences and prayers. Two fellows with guitars played tribute to which a few of us danced. I got Anna's young brother, who had become mentally disabled by a motorcycle accident, to join me in a simplified waltz.

The next day, Theresa sent a personal email expressing her appreciation for my presence, saying she'd been "deeply moved" that I'd come. That day I was restless, thinking of Anna, the way she died, the fact she was my age. She had suffered 10 years with early onset dementia prior to passing away. That night when I went to bed I'd pretty much moved on to thoughts of everyday minutia, but before the sun rose, before the light in the window tipped the circadian clock into daytime, something happened.

I awoke to pressure on my back, on my shoulders. Someone was there, next to me in bed! Not some*thing*, but some*one*, gently but firmly pressing as I lay on my side. I felt no temperature change, the covers had not moved. My instant thought was 'INTRUDER'! Simultaneously my heart rate shot up. I tried to scream but I couldn't make the scream go any farther than my chest. The muscles seemed to have clamped down on anything that wanted to move, like the mammogram machine that takes no prisoners and permits not one micrometer for inhaling.

The pressure remained, while I remained frozen in fear and wonder for another long moment. (Was it 5 seconds? 10? eternity?) Then as quickly as it came, it left.

It wasn't just *not there* anymore.

It *left*.

The next day I began to rationalize. Was it a dream? Surely science would explain the phenomenon in such light, or by some other well founded principle of physics. By the end of the day however my rational mind could not settle for the material explanation. I'd been aware of too much of the conscious world during the experience for it to be a fabrication of the dream world: the sound of the white noise device on the night stand, the feel of the comforter around my neck, the sensation of my own labored breathing. The sensory part of it was undeniable. Someone had visited and given me a hug that said, "I remember too."

Cold as the Grave

Theresa Davis

I opened my eyes to the still, cold, dark of the grave. Henry had finally made good on his promise to see me dead.

There was no way that my husband Henry should have been able to find me, but somehow he had. I had taken the first train out of town when I'd fled, and changed trains and directions in several larger cities before ultimately boarding The Rocket out of Union Station in Chicago getting off the train in Rock Island, Illinois.

I made my way across the river into Iowa. There I'd settled in and made a new life for myself north of the Quad Cities in LeClaire, Iowa, a quaint little river town. I thought I'd escaped him.

The nightmare I'd thought was over when I escaped on that humid summer night had begun again tonight and with a cold vengeance.

When I'd gone to answer the knock on the door, I'd expected Mrs. McAllister, my landlady, who was coming to share my supper. We made a point of dining together and listening to the radio a couple of times a week. She didn't have any family of her own left, and she considered me a kind of daughter. She was lonely and very kind to me, and I enjoyed her company.

I was surprised that she was so early, but figured she wanted to give herself plenty of time with the snow coming down so heavily. I crossed the living room to the front door, while Bing Crosby, on the radio in the corner crooned about his dreams for a white Christmas. I flung open the door with a smile because if Bing were anywhere near here, he would be getting his wish.

Imagine my surprise when Henry pushed his way inside. I scrambled away from him, putting the sofa between us.

"No kiss for your long lost husband, Em?"

He stalked me, but I kept circling around the overstuffed couch.

"What are you doing here, Henry? What do you want?"

"You were never a fool, Em. Don't start acting like one now. You know why I'm here. I've come to take back what's mine, and I must say I'm very displeased with you. You've made things very difficult for me and you're going to have to be punished for that."

"Why do you want a woman who doesn't want you? You're not the man I married. He was a kind gentle man who would never raise a hand to me. I don't even know who you are any more."

Henry had gone off to fight the Nazis in the war and had gotten involved with the black market in Europe. He had succeeded in that unwholesome world and had turned into a power hungry and avaricious man.

"That Henry was a sad pathetic loser. I came back from the war a strong man, a powerful man. I know what I want and I do what I have to do to get it. No one is going to take from me what's mine."

"I'm not a piece of property, Henry. I was your wife, not your slave."

"You made vows to me, Em. Do you remember?"

I nodded, unable to speak, and he continued, "You promised to love, honor and obey me, until death parts us. Do you remember that?"

Tears threatened to flood my eyes as I choked out, "I do."

He pointed to the floor beside him and demanded, "Get over here, wife, and stop all this foolishness. I'm taking you back to where you belong."

I shook my head and raced to the cellar door. Wrenching

it open, I raced down the narrow wooden steps to the cellar and hid beneath the stairs.

"Damn you, Emily, don't you dare run from me."

His feet pounded on every step as he slowly, deliberately came down the stairs. I clutched the old cavalry pistol to my chest. Mrs. McAllister had insisted that I take her father's gun to keep myself safe. She'd said that a woman living alone needs a big dog, or a loaded gun, possibly both, until a good man comes along to see to her safety.

I'd never imagined that I'd need to use that gun, but at that moment in time I was relieved and grateful that she'd forced me to learn how to load and fire it.

༺༻

The last thing I remembered, before waking to cold dark oblivion was clinging to that gun with my heart racing in my chest beneath the basement stairs.

I'd always thought death would be peaceful, but my head throbbed with pain. I came to the realization that maybe Henry hadn't killed me after all.

The inside of the car was dark. The snow had blanketed the windows so I must have been unconscious for quite a while. I gingerly touched my forehead and my hand came back red with blood from where it must have made contact with the unforgiving hardness of the steering wheel.

My teeth began chattering, I didn't know if it was from the bitter cold, reaction from the accident, fear of Henry appearing again, or the sight of my own blood, but I knew I had to move and get somewhere warm and out of the snow. I was aware that people succumbed to the cold when the temperatures were even higher than they were outside.

Wishing I'd grabbed a more substantial coat, I stepped out into the blizzard and scrambled back onto Stagecoach Trail.

I looked back towards the Buick Roadmaster and could barely see it through the driving snow even though I knew it was only a few feet away from where I stood. I was on foot, in a blinding whiteness with an aching head and fear for my life. If Henry didn't manage to kill me, Mother Nature just might.

I jumped and screamed, when the deep voice said from right behind me, "Are you all right, ma'am? Is there anything I can do for you?"

I slowly turned and a large figure loomed into my view. I swallowed my fear and replied, "I've had an accident. I slid off the road."

I needed to get off the road and away from Henry's car

before he hunted me down, but I wasn't going to tell that to this strange man.

The large man said, "My name is Raymond Hultquist, ma'am, you can call me Ray. My folks John and Edna Hultquist live just the other side of Glendale cemetery over yonder. Follow me and I'll take you to their house. You'll be out of the weather, and Ma will get you warmed up and fed, after she bandages that gash on your forehead.

"Pa will bring round the tractor and pull your car out in the morning after the snow stops falling."

I smiled and replied, "Thank you, Ray. I certainly do appreciate your help. I'm Emily Maroni. You can call me Emily."

He started trudging off into the cemetery, saying, "It's real nice to meet you, Emily. You're mighty lucky."

I certainly didn't feel particularly lucky, but at least I was still alive. A lot of people would think twice before venturing through a cemetery at night, but I had so much more to worry about from the living than I did from the dead. So I had no qualms about following Ray into the night.

"What are you doing out here in this miserable weather? Although I must say I'm really glad that you are out here, Ray, I don't know if I'd ever be able to find my way to safety on my own in this white out. I've never known it to snow so hard like this, but then I just moved to these parts this summer. Where I'm from we barely get a couple of inches of snow in an entire season, certainly not a couple of feet in one night."

"It is mighty dangerous being out in this weather. People tell lots of stories around these parts about knowing of people getting all turned around in a blizzard and not making it to shelter. They say those folks are found frozen to death even though they're a few feet from their own back door."

I shivered, not sure if from cold or realization of my close call, and plodded after Ray into the whipping white of the snowstorm.

I tucked my hands into my sleeves in a vain effort to try to keep them warm and kept my head down trying to keep as much of the snow from stinging my eyes as I could. My efforts were not particularly effective.

My feet were blocks of ice as I stumbled across the terrain, keeping my eyes focused on the Ray's knees that were the lowest part of him I could see. The rest of his legs were hidden beneath the ever-deepening blanket of snow on the ground. Since he was a good six inches taller than me, I was slogging through snow hitting me around mid-thigh.

He walked slowly and steadily and I still had a hard time keeping up with him.

Ray must have been keeping to the path through the cemetery; otherwise, I would have surely tripped over the lower monuments. I don't know how he could tell where the path actually was because you couldn't see much more than a few feet in front of you, but he seemed to walk on like there were no hindrances to battle.

After what seemed like hours trudging through the snow, I stopped and gasped, "Ray, please, I can't go on." He turned to me and said, "You must keep moving. It won't be long now. We're almost there."

I shook my head and whined, "I can't feel my feet. My face is frozen. You just go on without me."

"No. I won't leave you. You think you're cold, but this is nothing like the cold of that battlefield in the Ardennes. You felt as if your blood froze solid in your veins. And there was no hope for shelter and a roaring fire. You just hunkered down in your foxhole with your buddies and hoped that the German snipers wouldn't find you in their crosshairs.

"And then in the dead of night in that unrelenting cold, you prayed that you would end up prey to the German guns just so you wouldn't have to deal with the miserable cold. You've scarce been out here for an hour, imagine day after unending day, with the dead and dying all around you and the unceasing cold, that God-forsaken cold sapping your will to live."

Ray stopped talking and I saw the horror of what he'd been through in his dark tortured eyes. I reached a trembling hand towards him, saying, "I'm so sorry, I can't imagine how horrible that must have been for you."

Before I could touch him, he turned away, saying, "Keep walking, ma'am. We're almost there, maybe five minutes more. You can do it."

I tucked my hands back into my sleeves and plodded after Ray before he disappeared into the blowing snow leaving me alone with no one for company except the dead sleeping beneath the unrelenting blanket of snow.

I staggered against the gate at the far side of the cemetery and asked, "How much farther, Ray?"

"Almost there."

I sped up when I thought I heard a voice out in the snowstorm calling my name.

Ray looked surprised when I came up beside him and insisted, "We need to hurry."

He looked down at me and asked, "Is there a problem?"

I shook my head, and he stopped, and said, "We're not going any farther until you tell me what's wrong. What made you drive out into a blizzard? I don't want to see my folks in danger. I don't want to see you in danger. So tell me, what you're frightened of and tell me now?"

Heaving a heavy sigh, I admitted, "My husband Henry Maroni has come into town to kill me. I ran away from him last August and he's managed to find me."

Ray straightened and looked back towards the cemetery with narrowed eyes. He growled, "Henry Maroni. Well, don't that just beat all?"

"You know Henry?"

With a curt nod, he turned and said, "You could say that. It's just a little bit more."

I finally saw the old clapboard farmhouse loom up out of the whiteness. The thought of being out of the wind and the snow and especially the cold gave me a brief burst of energy. I raced ahead of Ray and reached the back porch and pounded on the door.

The door was opened by an older, thinner version of Ray and he called, "Edna, come quick. There's some poor woman found her way to our door on this miserable night. Get the kettle to boiling "

He helped me inside and I turned to thank Ray for

leading me to shelter, but he was no longer in view.

Edna came bustling over and drew me over to a rocking chair beside the fire. She cooed, "Oh, you poor little lamb, you're just frozen to the bone. We'll get you settled here and get you bundled up and then I'll make you a nice cup of tea. Then I'll fetch you a nice dry nightie to change into." I let her take care of me and feeling safe and starting to thaw out, I slipped into sleep.

The smell of bacon woke me from my slumber and I crawled out from under the pile of blankets that Mrs. Hultquist had covered me with.

Rubbing my eyes I followed my nose and walked into the kitchen, where I found Mr. and Mrs. Hultquist sitting at the wooden table eating a farmer's breakfast of scrambled eggs, fried potatoes, and bacon.

Mrs. Hultquist leapt to her feet, saying, "You're looking much better this morning. Sit down and I'll fix you a plate."

I sat in the chair she'd motioned me to and said, "Thank you. I feel much better than when I arrived."

My stomach grumbled, and I blushed. Mr. Hultquist

chuckled, "Hurry, Edna, the poor girl is starving."

My blush deepened, and she made a shooing motion with her hand at him, saying, "You're embarrassing the poor girl, John. Now you behave yourself."

She turned to me and soothed, "Don't you pay him no never mind, dear. If you hadn't dropped off so quickly, I'd have given you some supper."

Putting a plate piled high with food, she added, "Now you eat up, dear. Don't be shy. We've got plenty more if you want it."

I smiled, saying, "Thank you."

Since I was so hungry I started eating without another word. The food was delicious and in no time I had cleaned my plate.

I set down my fork and asked, "Is there any chance you could take me down into the Cities to the train station?"

Edna asked, "Is that where you were headed last night in the snowstorm?"

"Yes, ma'am, I was."

John asked, "How were you traveling? You surely weren't walking into the Cities. That's not quite twenty miles to the station."

I had taken Henry's Roadmaster when I'd fled into the snow because he'd blocked in my car. I didn't want to go back to my house in case he was still there, and I didn't think it would be safe to go back to Henry's car.

I smiled a little sheepishly and admitted, "I'd borrowed a car and drove it off the road. I'd just as soon not have to go back and tell them I've wrecked their car."

Which was partly true, I didn't want to tell Henry anything, much less admitting I'd wrecked his car.

Mr. Hultquist looked suspicious and asked, "What's your name, young lady?"

"I'm Emily Maroni. I rent a house from Mrs. McAllister out on Stagecoach Trail."

Mrs. Hultquist mused, "Maroni. I don't recall anyone named Maroni living hereabouts, but that name sure does sound familiar to me."

"Of course, it does, Edna, that's the name of the man that Ray was going to see on the day he died, at least that's what that fellow Joe VanHorbeck from his outfit told us at the funeral. Henry Maroni was the man they thought was stealing the medicine from the army for the black market. Joe said they couldn't prove Henry killed Ray, but that's what they all believed."

I yelped, "Died! What do you mean, died?"

She replied, "Our son Ray was killed over in France. The last letter he ever wrote to us arrived about a month after we buried him over in Glendale Cemetery."

Shaking my head, I insisted, "Ray led me from my wrecked car, through the cemetery, to your door. I would have died if he hadn't shown up and brought me down here."

Mr. Hultquist said, "That's not funny, young lady."

I shook my head. "I swear to you. I'm not trying to be funny. The man I followed down here told me his name was Ray Hultquist. He very strongly resembled you, sir. I can't believe he wasn't real."

"Get her bundled up, Edna. I'll show her the truth of the situation."

With shaking hands, Mrs. Hultquist bundled me up in layers of warm clothes, and a sturdy pair of boots. I soon was hiking back into the cemetery following Mr. Hultquist.

Turning off the main path, Mr. Hultquist stopped suddenly, and roared, "What the devil is going on here?"

I looked to where he was staring and saw Henry appearing to be lying beside a tombstone that read, "Raymond A. Hultquist Beloved Son Born – February 10, 1928 Died - April 10, 1945"

That's when darkness claimed me and I sank into the snow at the feet of Mr. Hultquist.

I woke back up on the settee in the Hultquist living

room. The county sheriff and Mrs. McAllister were there along with the Hultquists.

Noticing I was awake, the sheriff asked, "What can you tell me about last night, Mrs. Maroni?"

I told them everything starting with running away from Henry last summer through Ray leading me through the storm to the Hultquist's home.

When I'd finished, the sheriff ran his hand through his thinning hair and said, "Well, ma'am, I've got to tell you that your husband Henry was found dead in Glendale Cemetery. Somehow, his feet were buried in the soil of Raymond Hultquist's grave. How they got buried in that frozen ground I can't begin to tell you, but it's a fact that they were solidly planted there.

"If I was a fanciful fellow, I'd say Ray reached up out of the grave and grabbed hold of your husband's feet and held onto him until he froze to death. But we all know that that's just not possible."

I looked towards the picture of Ray that his parents had hanging above their mantle and smiled, sending him a silent thank you for saving my life not once on that snowy evening, but twice.

Author's Note: Raymond, John, and Edna Hultquist, and Ida Mae McAllister are all interred in the Glendale Cemetery in LeClaire, Iowa.

Ghost of a Life

Jannette LaRoche

"I've really missed you, Mom. Dad has too. But we're all going to be together again soon. I know you won't understand. I got this letter. I'll read it to you."

The young woman's fingers were stiff with cold as she fumbled around in her pocket, but she managed to retrieve the envelope and unfold the paper inside.

"Dear Sarah. I know I can never thank you enough for what you've done, but I have to at least try. After you left the bank they only had to let one other person go. Troy was laid off, but I was able to keep my job. If it wasn't for you I don't know what I would have done. I didn't want anyone to know, but my oldest son was diagnosed with leukemia last year. Without my insurance I would never have been able to take care of him. He's in remission now, and it's all because of you. I hope you are doing well and know that you will always be a hero in my eyes."

Sarah sniffed back tears as she finished reading. "I had no idea, Mom. I was only thinking of myself. I needed to get out and never even considered what might happen to the people I left behind. But now I see I can do some good before I go. Daddy doesn't have much time left. The doctors gave him six months and that was five months ago. When he's gone I'll be all alone. So I've decided to try to help as many people as I can and then follow him."

Having said it out loud, Sarah felt more convinced this was the right decision. "I'll see you soon." She kissed the gravestone and turned to leave.

"Did you really mean that?"

Sarah had thought she was alone in the cemetery, and the appearance of the man so close by startled her.

"I'm sorry. I didn't mean to eavesdrop. I was just visiting someone myself and happened to overhear." He smiled at her warmly, and Sarah felt her cheeks flush. Not only had this man learned her very private plans, he was also exceedingly handsome in an old-fashioned way. He wore a dark grey suit, complete with hankie in the pocket, and carried a fedora in one hand. A red scarf wrapped around his neck but he wore no coat despite the March chill.

She realized she was staring and looked quickly away, but could not come up with a single thing to say to him.

"Your mother?" he asked. At her nod he went on. "I

lost my mother several years ago myself. The pain never really goes away, but it becomes bearable. That's the way of life. And death."

"I'm sorry for your loss." Sarah regained her composure enough to risk another glance. He was still smiling, but off into the distance.

"So did you mean what you said?"

His arrogance suddenly infuriated her, and Sarah found the strength to stand up tall and defend her decision, even though it was none of his business.

"Yes. I did. There's nothing left for me in this world, or won't be after my father's gone. I have no future, but I can give a future to others in my place."

"That's a very noble way to die."

She wasn't sure if he was sincere or disingenuous. "Thank you."

"Of course, dying is easy. Living is what's hard."

"And how would you know?"

He stared at her for several moments before responding. "I know a few things. I'm Carl, by the way. It was nice to meet you, Sarah. I hope to see you around again sometime."

He sauntered away toward the trees and she was left staring and speechless. The nerve of him. And yet... Oh, well. No point in standing around wondering what might have been. She had plans and had to get to them.

Sarah felt much lighter after delivering all of her father's old paint supplies to the craft store. She scanned the flyer they gave her and noted she could make a contribution through them to donate supplies to area teachers. There would be quite a bit of money after life insurance and selling the house.

She walked the few blocks down Cody Street to the steakhouse where she now worked. The owners, friends of her father's, had been very generous in not only giving her a job but also letting her set her schedule around her dad's doctor appointments. She smiled as always at the collection of cut-off ties and the bullet holes in the tin ceiling. This had been one of her favorite restaurants as a kid, and she was pleased to find the atmosphere no different.

"Haven't seen you smile in some time, darlin'." Loretta had been a waitress there for so many years she'd earned the right to give her customers and coworkers nicknames.

"I've gotten a lot accomplished already today. It feels good."

"You know if there's anything Mike and I can do to help…"

"Thanks. Right now I'm just working on clearing out the small stuff. I'll be sure to let you know if I need Mike's muscles later on."

Her shift passed uneventfully, as did her visit with her dad at the nursing home. He was having a good day, able to stay awake for nearly an hour before the pain became too much and he had to request more medication. Sarah couldn't tell him her plan, of course, but she shared little details of her day to keep his mind off the pain.

The cemetery was just a couple of blocks down on Iowa Drive, and on impulse she stopped. It was crazy to think Carl would be there so late in the evening, and even crazier that she hoped he would be. But he knew. He knew what she planned to do and didn't try to talk her out of it or call an ambulance to take her away to the nut house. She was desperately lonely, and Carl seemed like someone she could trust. He just had an air about him.

She saw him before he saw her this time. Still wearing his suit he sat peacefully on a bench looking out over the headstones.

"Do you work here or something?"

"Why would you say that?" He didn't seem surprised by her sudden appearance or odd question.

"You're here again, and you're dressed up."

"You're here as well."

"I just stopped in to see my dad at the nursing home

up the road."

"He's ill?"

"Only got a couple of weeks left. Pancreatic cancer."

"And you're very sad."

"Well, yeah. I don't have any other family left except a crazy uncle out in California."

"No husband? Children?"

Sarah couldn't stop the snort of disgust from escaping her throat. "No possibility of that. Not anymore."

"I don't understand," he said with a slight frown, the lines on his forehead wrinkling in concentration.

Sarah sighed heavily and dropped onto the seat next to him. "I had a boyfriend. We talked about getting married but he didn't want to be official about it. That's what he said, anyway. Then a few months ago I got a call while I was at work—my dad telling me he was going to die soon. I left work and rushed home to get packed and go visit him. That's when I found my so-called boyfriend in bed with my so-called best friend. I lost the only people left in my life within the space of less than an hour.

"I couldn't handle it anymore. I had to get away. I packed what I could into my car and came home. I called into work and told them I was leaving. Went back just one time to get my last paycheck and the rest of my stuff. I was such a coward I did it while she was at work. I couldn't face either one of them ever again."

"But something good came of it," Carl prompted.

"Yeah. The bank where I worked had just announced they were going to have to lay off two people. Troy should have been fired long before, but Beth was a hard worker raising three kids on her own. Her husband left her just after their daughter was born. Poor lady. She never complained though. She thinks I left for her sake. It made me realize how much we go through life worrying about ourselves, never stopping to think about anyone else. It was like divine inspiration. I couldn't save myself from the crap my life had become, but I could help others."

Carl shook his head, not as if disagreeing, just in a sad, defeated way.

"I thought that at one time myself. I thought the people I loved would be better off without me. The problem with dying is that it cuts off possibilities. It's only a solution to the people doing the dying, not those they leave behind."

"Lucky for me I don't have anyone to leave behind."

"How do you know? Maybe in your future you meet someone new, have children, save a person's life. You'll be leaving all those people behind, even if you haven't met them yet."

"I've made up my mind." Sarah was annoyed, more at herself for getting to know this man than at what he was saying. If she had to chose right now she could go through with it. If she made a new friend, though, would she still be able to?

"Look, I have to go. It was very nice to meet you and I wish you a long and happy life."

She was several yards away before his voice stopped her. "Have you considered the library?"

"What?"

"The local library. You said you wanted to do some good. They could use it."

"Sure. Thanks. I'll look into it." He was still sitting where she found him when she pulled away.

"Do you have any information about planned giving?" Sarah had delivered the entire contents of her parents' den to the library. It took four trips in her small car, but the library was now the owner of an immense collection of westerns and romance novels, as well as a variety of nonfiction books covering nearly every subject available.

"Yes. We have an endowment through the Community Foundation. We accept cash, stocks, IRA contributions, or anything else you would want to give. Do you know someone planning an estate?"

"My father." The words came out around a lump in her throat. Sarah felt she should be used to it by now, but saying it out loud still hurt.

"My condolences." The head librarian was a sharply dressed woman who conveyed both professionalism and compassion in equal parts. "Why don't I get you a cup of coffee while I find the paperwork."

An hour later, Sarah was headed to the steakhouse to report for work and put in her two weeks' notice. After hearing her story and learning her background in accounting, the librarian offered Sarah a job on the spot. She couldn't say quite why she accepted. The hours and pay were certainly better, but it's not like she was looking for anything more than something to get her through the next few months. The idea of working at the library just appealed to her. She spent her shift humming tunelessly and thinking of Carl. How had he known?

By the time she got off work at 10:30 that night she couldn't justify a trip to the cemetery. Besides, no one would be out there that late. She spent a restless night, waiting for morning and the chance to talk with Carl again. Her dreams were scattered, images of people she had known throughout the years flashing and fading away, moments that seemed trivial at the time replayed in bright spotlight, and over and over again the feeling of emptiness when she had lost her grandmother and mother.

The sun gleamed off the white marble stones as she wandered through their rows early the next day. She searched, but could not find Carl. Of course, why would he be there? Two chance meetings certainly didn't mean anything, held no promises for the future. Sarah knew that, but could not stem the disappointment that welled up inside.

After lunch with Dad she tried once more, and was overjoyed to see him waiting once more on the same bench.

"I wanted to say thank you, for the advice about the library." She told him about the job offer and her excitement about working at the library. "It's even better than what I was making at the bank in Iowa City. And everyone there is so nice and friendly."

"I've always loved libraries."

They talked for some time about books and people and their favorite things to do when they were kids. Eventually she got up the courage to ask if he'd like to have dinner with her.

"I can't. Not tonight."

"Maybe another time?" She was let down, and the feeling was foreign. For so many months now she'd had nothing to look forward to, and therefore no disappointment. Was it better that way?

The phone rang late that night. Sarah visited the cemetery as soon as she was finished signing forms and talking to doctors and funeral directors and all the other people who make a living off the inevitableness of dying.

"He's coming here then?" Carl stood close to Sarah. Close but not touching, and she realized just how much she'd missed human contact lately.

"He'll be buried next to my mother."

"And what about you? Will you be coming here soon?"

"I... I don't know anymore."

Carl smiled in a sad way. "I have something to show you. I think you're ready to see it now."

He led her to a worn headstone on the far edge of the cemetery. It read, "Carl Jacobs. 1898-1924. Beloved Son and Brother."

"Was he a relative of yours?" She already knew the answer somehow, but refused to admit what she should have known all along.

He shook his head slowly and unwound the scarf from his neck to reveal a horrible thick bruise encircling it.

"You asked me when we first met how I knew dying was easy and life was hard. I know because I've been on both sides. My life was hard, my dying was easy, but this...

This waiting is worse than anything. I've watched my parents come here and felt my siblings sorrow, only to go through it all over again when they died and their children suffered. But they all moved on, because they'd lived their lives. There are no shortcuts, no easy way out.

"When I saw you that first day, I couldn't bear the thought of you ending up like me. You have such life within you, if only you would let it free."

Sarah dropped to the ground and touched the stone, hoping somehow it was what was not real. Carl knelt beside and placed his hand over hers. The two became one as his flesh seemed to slide into hers. She shivered.

"I don't want to leave you." Her voice was small and desperate. She had finally found a reason to live and her reason had been dead nearly a hundred years.

"Then don't."

"I can stay here like you?"

"No." He moved his hand to caress the space just beyond her cheek. It felt like a warm wind across her skin. "No, not like me. You can stay here like you. Like you making friends and falling in love. You having children and grandchildren. You making a difference in the world in the way only you can. You living life, a real life, not just the ghost of a life. And I will be here whenever you need me."

The casket was lowered into the ground. The eyes of those standing around the grave were moist with unshed tears. She had told them not to cry for her. "Cry for yourself, if you must. Dying is easy. Life is hard. But it's worth it."

Her granddaughter excused herself to search the grounds. She had been particularly close to the old woman, and would miss her wisdom. On impulse, she headed to the far side of the cemetery, remembering an impossible story her grandmother had told her once when she was having an exceptionally awful time dealing with life. She found the grave, its words nearly illegible.

"Look after my grandma, you hear?"

The wind whistled through the leaves, and she could almost hear it say, "I always have."

The True Nature of Evil

Jannette LaRoche

"Are you sure this is safe, Chet?"

He stopped and turned around. "I know this is scary, Abby. I won't blame you if you decide to turn back."

She drew in a deep breath. "No. I promised I would help."

He tucked a stray hair behind her ear. "You are so brave and beautiful."

If her heart had pounded hard in her chest before, it doubled its intensity now. "When this is all over..." Her voice came out as barely a whisper, and she tried again. "When this is all over will we still be friends?"

He grabbed her hands and pulled them up to his chest. "More than friends. I promise."

If the whole situation hadn't been so crazy to start with this might have set warning bells off in her brain. Only in her wildest dreams could she ever have imagined standing under the moonlight, holding hands with Chet. Not even in her dreams would she have guessed this would happen just before they were about to break into the craft shop.

Before last week she didn't think Chet even knew her name. Chet Williams, football player and president of student council, was the type of person all the guys wanted to be and all the girls wanted to be with. Abby Jackson was... not.

She was not athletic, not beautiful, not popular. She wasn't the kind of person who got picked on. She was the kind of person no one ever gave a thought about, not even a blip on their radar. So it was a complete surprise when Chet sat down beside her in the school library.

"Hey, Abby. I was wondering if you could do me a favor."

She agreed immediately. Another thing she was not was immune to Chet's charm.

"I'm looking for books on strange stuff—ghosts, demons, the occult. I'm afraid old eagle-eyes Mrs. Hartwick might get the wrong idea if I asked her."

She showed him the section and assumed that would be the end of it. But he caught up to her after school, right in the middle of the hallway where everyone could see.

"I didn't find what I needed. Is there any chance you could go with me to the public library and help me look some more?"

The public library also failed to produce the answers he wanted, and it nearly broke her heart to see him so defeated.

"I could help you look online if you let me know what you need."

He pulled his chair closer and leaned in, his eyes darting back and forth before he wet his lips and asked, "Do you believe in ghosts?"

"I don't know. In theory, I guess. I've never actually seen one."

"I have." Chet's eyes were large and round, his jaw and fists clenched tight, his face ashen. "It started a few weeks ago. He's been following me everywhere. I think he wants to take me over. I don't know what to do. I'm really freaked out."

She didn't doubt him for a minute. They searched through every source they could get hold of, print and online, movies and TV shows and song lyrics. They held a séance and consulted a Ouija board. At last they had a glimmer of hope.

"Robert Kramer lived in the house on Cody that is the craft store now. He was murdered by his lover's husband at Steamboat Landing near where the Buffalo Bill Museum is now. And he's buried in Glendale Cemetery. His spirit has to be attached to one of those places. We'll have to try the ritual at each one until we free him to move on."

Chet suggested they start at the craft store, since they didn't know exactly where the murder had taken place and it was easier and safer than digging up a grave. And so here they were.

Chet kissed her forehead lightly before turning to the seldom used back door. He retrieved his library card from his back pocket and began shimmying it around the lock. In far less time than Abby would have expected the handle turned in his fist and the door opened into a dark and crowded room.

They entered silently, the beams of their flashlights bounced off the random assortment of objects in the room, creating fearsome looking shadows. Chet led the way confidently through the ground level and up the steep stairs. Abby followed a few steps behind, her senses, heightened by fear, picking up every sound and movement.

When she reached the top she saw a beam of light lying against the floor and followed it to find Chet's flashlight discarded.

"Chet?" she called softly.

"He's here." Chet appeared at her side, eyes wild and body shaking like a leaf in a storm. "I can feel him. He's so much stronger here. I don't think I can hold him off."

"Don't worry, Chet. I'll take care of you."

"Aaaagghh!" Chet's body twitched and jerked for a moment then went completely still. Abby reached out for him, and when he raised his eyes to hers she saw his face was bloody. She stepped back, knocking a bowl of beads to the floor. Chet took a step toward her, one leg dragging behind him. His hands, also covered in blood, reached for her. And she fainted.

Laughter beckoned her forth from the blackness.

"Oh man, that was precious." Not Chet's voice.

Cautiously Abby opened her eyes. It was bright, far too bright. She blinked and forced the world into focus. She saw the lens of a video camera and followed it to Jason Maynard, who was leering at her viciously. She rolled her head to the side and found Alex Dawson handing wet wipes to Chet, who was wiping fake blood from his face.

"What's going on? Chet, are you okay?"

The three laughed again, the sound slicing through her skin and into her soul like a thousand poison dipped daggers.

"Man, you weren't kidding. This girl is gull-i-ble."

Realization sunk in and stiffened her spine. "You guys are pigs."

"Don't take it too hard," Chet said. He offered a hand to help her to her feet but she ignored it. "You'll be famous on YouTube."

Abby gathered the shards of her dignity and wrapped them around her like a cloak. "I thought the ghost of Robert Kramer was evil, but I was wrong. You're evil and someday you'll get what you deserve." The boys hooted at this, but she retrieved her flashlight and made her way down the stairs and out the door without another word.

"That was awesome, Chet. You sure do know how to pull a good one."

The boys left the store and went down to the river where they congratulated themselves with a round of beer while they recapped the highlights of their prank. It occurred to Chet briefly that they were close to site where Robert Kramer was murdered, but he put it out of his mind.

"Dude, I think you got us some skanky beer," Alex complained as he drained his can.

"Don't be a wuss." Jason popped another open to show how little he cared.

"No, he's right. I feel really weird." Chet wiped a bead of sweat from his forehead.

"Are you two girls telling me you can't handle a single beer anymore?"

"Not sick," Alex gasped. "Just weird. Wrong somehow."

Jason opened his mouth to let another insult fly, but the words stuck in his mouth. His body went rigid and his eyes fixed on a point somewhere beyond the others.

"What is it?"

Jason raised a shaking hand to point. The others turned slowly, but they knew, deep in their souls, what they were about to find.

The figure stepped out of the darkness, his left leg, twisted at an impossible angle, trailed on the floor yet somehow held his weight. Thick dark liquid oozed from a long slash across his face and trailed down his arms until it dripped from his fingers. He opened his arms as if to embrace the terrified boys.

They looked into his eyes and saw the true nature of evil.

And then they saw no more.

Scourge of the River

Ellen Tsagaris

It was dusk on a cold, fall day.

I had just moved to LeClaire, and was reading the local paper, bought from a tiny, family owned river front pharmacy/soda fountain that had been in town forever. I had just come from San Jose, taking a job with the local paper here, trying to find old friends from the cities where I had grown up, trying to forget a bad divorce that played itself out on the shores of the Pacific.

The old green river pilot's house sat on a small hill on Cody Road, named for Buffalo Bill, our most famous citizen. I could sit in the room on the top floor that looked like an old attic, drink coffee from our local café, and write about the latest business to close or open, the latest scandal involving one of the states attorneys in the Cities, the latest economic crisis threatening our biggest local employer, an aluminum plant, or our federal munitions factory.

It was quiet that late autumn afternoon, but I was uneasy. Strange things had been happening since I'd moved into the pilot's house. I'd had dreams, nightmares, really, of a woman in an elegant black dress from the 19th century, with a pale face and large, luminous sad eyes, beckoning me, right up to the table where I now sat in the old attic room. I hadn't had a chance to clean out this room. My job was relatively stress free, and running the local paper's editorial section did require some local travel, but I found I was often very tired, and the winding, uphill path to my front door often wore me out. In my dream, the woman often met me at my front door, held it open, and led me in. Sometimes, she took me by the hand to usher me over my threshold, and her touch was cold, cold as marble.

I had other "day" nightmares or visions when I went to our local market on the hill, especially around the meat counter, and when I looked at old books in our many antique shops, I kept finding books about Jack the Ripper, and old tomes and penny broadsides of a similar set of ripper/slasher murders that took place over 100 years ago in this very neighborhood, and in the nearby cities. Everyone thought some hobo or river rat had committed the murders. They stopped, eventually, a few years after the Ripper murders stopped in London.

In my visions and dreams, the woman always pointed when I held the books, and she seemed to glide up the stairs and disappear at the attic door.

I liked the attic room where I now sat; it had big cabbage rose wallpaper, and a rug, and an old toy box. The box was full of toys, riverboats, blocks, little horses and soldiers, and a big, very old doll with a bisque head and staring glass eyes. Her body was jointed, even double-jointed, and could assume a contortionist's position. Her clothes were long gone, and the elastics that held the doll together were loose, so that she seemed to assume even more interesting gymnastic poses. I thought of trying to get her restored, or of taking the toys to the local antique dealers to be appraised, but I was loathe, for some reason, to remove them from their old, carved toy chest.

Lack of sleep was really affecting me; I heard windows rattling when they were closed, and footsteps when I knew I was alone. I thought I saw the doll move in the trunk, and at first dismissed it; she was just getting looser in her elastic, and slipping on the pile of toys which she crowned in the box. Only her head seemed not to move.

Then, was it me?

Horror!

The doll opened her eyes!

I wasn't asleep or dreaming, now, and while I tried to recover from one horror, another accosted me. The door opened, and I knew I had closed it. A small woman, nearly translucent in her paleness, with a lace cap and dark hair drawn up in a chignon, stood before me. She was sad, not really frightening, but she startled me. She took the chair across from me; had I seen her move from the door? She seemed to glide, and not to be of this world.

I began to ask her questions.

"Who are you?"

"How did you get in; the door was locked?"

"I know you; you live in my house," she answered. "You know my story, but you have not read it yet. "Pick up the doll, and gently, very gently, lift off her head. Don't be afraid, it will give easily."

As if in a trance, I did as she asked. I was terrified, but somehow believed she wouldn't harm me. I carefully took out the doll, and lifted off her bisque head. The glass eyes of blue closed again. Inside her body, her head had rested on a roll of very old paper, yellow and brittle with age, covered in spidery, faded brown writing?

Ink?

Blood, I later thought.

These were tied with faded black, silk ribbons.

"Untie the ribbons, " my ghostly pale visitor bade me.

"Read; I am dead; I have all the time in the world. You

don't, and I would have you publish my story, publish these words."

I did as she asked, and below is the story she told in her scroll.

⁓⁓

A bluish, early morning light cast rays through the barred nursery windows, leaving patterns like blue icicles on the gray rug. There was no sound in the room, only the light tapping of a branch against the window. I sat in a white painted rocker, and I gazed at the barred pattern on the rug.

I was finally alone that morning. Bess was at the market on Green Street shopping; Jim Salt, our handyman, was with this sick mother. And my husband? My husband, Dr. Michael Anton Jones was in the cities, in Davenport, at his medical office, consulting with other wives of our circle, wives who could do what I could not, produce another riverboat skipper or captain of local industry to serve our growing river town.

I could see Michael Anton properly patting soft hands as frail and dainty as birds, reassuring women about the "wonderful" miracle about to befall them, all the while as enchanting as the Prince of Wales in far away London.

The newspaper I had been reading dropped from my hands and fell as a veil on the hearth rug. There was a huge fireplace before me–built into the oldest part of the house. Originally, the house had secret passages, carved in place some 40 years before when LeClaire was a stop for the Underground Railroad.

Though it was still early fall, it was a cold morning, and a wind came off the river, sharp as the point of an anchor. I'd kindled a fire sometime earlier, and now the dying embers blended with the sapphire light from the windows so that the resulting shadows cast weird hieroglyphics about the room.

The nursery was supposed to be off-limits to me since we'd lost our first, and only, child five years earlier. Michael and the Chicago specialist he'd consulted thought it best. My constitution was delicate. Since, regrettably, I could have no more children, and since the nursery only stirred memories better forgotten, Michael gave Bess the keys and told her to get rid of them. But I kept some; Michael never knew how many there were; he didn't bother himself with domestic matters.

So, the nursery was kept shut-up but for my visits. Fine dust lay like a film over the crib and toys. Cobwebs shrouded everything else for the spiders were both fertile and industrious, interweaving their fine silk in a doll's hair, laying eggs in a turned-over Noah's Ark. The toy riverboat was now a ghost ship; it's crew made up of dead field mice and long-dead Polyphemus moths with brittle wings.

It was in the nursery that I spun my own webs and read the lurid broadsides and the sanitized stories of the papers my husband hid in the study—for I had other keys as well. He had a cousin in England who sent him the London Times, and he followed the horrific tales of the East Side Ripper with great alacrity. He never saw himself in the customers who frequented the unfortunate East End street walkers victimized by Ripper.

Even though Michael loved the saloon girls and ladies of the evening, those who prowled the riverfront on cold dusky evenings to earn a coin or two for room and board on Green Street, he never saw his soiled doves as part of the same flock as the Ripper victims so far across the ocean. He never thought our local Madame Fat Jennie Goofydonk head mistress of our local house of ill repute, Riverville, or the girls who worked as barmaids at the Unfaithful Mermaid, had anything in common with the dried out gin tarts and desperate women of Whitechapel, the Ripper's hometown.

And, even if they didn't, the entire community of our little town nestled on the banks of the Mississippi, as mighty as the Thames or any river, was fascinated. Many of our neighbors climbed the winding path to our green mansion, a former river pilot's home, to share a pipe and lurid story or two from the English papers.

But, I loved the Ripper stories, too.

I was honest about it.

I didn't blush and twitter away behind my lace caps and dust veils the way other women did when they were caught with a penny broadside or news clipping about old Leather Apron. I didn't pretend to faint and fan myself either, when Bess began to tell the latest stories, and Michael quickly shushed her lest I hear. I didn't have to worry, though, few people spoke to me. But, I loved Ripper; Ripper inspired me, and gave me ideas. I had to wonder why so many thought Ripper was a man.

Was it because Ripper was free to walk the streets alone at night? Didn't George Sand, the great female novelist, do the same dressed as a man?

Was it because Ripper was brave and fearless?

Wasn't Elizabeth I the same, or Boadicea, scourge of Rome, or Artemesia the Ancient Greek admiral, or Joan of Arc, or the Amazons? Was it because Ripper was clever and cunning? So many women shared the same trait. No, I thought Ripper might be a woman, one like me, a wife dishonored and diseased by a brutish, selfish husband and his filthy doxies, a woman set on revenge, who liked adventure, a woman like me. A woman who bided her times, and left stealthily when no one looked, a woman who had adventures and excursions no one suspected.

I planned my next excursion, my next hunt, you might say in the nursery. Ladies of my class were encouraged to hunt in the country. Delicate I might be, but riding was thought to be good exercise as well as part of a necessary education. I learned to wield a silver-bladed, tiny knife to hack off the ears of a mangled animal, and I was never too squeamish to watch the hunters eviscerate the hapless little fox when they divided their spoils.

For even, here, on the banks of Old Man River, the upper class staged a fox hunt now and then, as a nod to our English cousins. We were good Anglophiles, one and all. We loved to imitate all things British, even to the point that we mimicked English crimes. A few of Fat Jennie's girls had been found dead under a rock or two in one of our many parks, in the cellar of one of our merchants, along the banks of the river, with the gulls screaming over who would chew on her vitals.

Come to think of it, I knew a lot about all kinds of anatomy. When Bess snored by the hob after one of her medicinal rounds of bourbon, and our handyman was away on errands, I used the key to the study and browsed among my husband's medical books. I'd always been an insatiable reader; I'd always felt more myself with a volume in my hand. I loved the feel of the book, the rich, sensual, almost masculine smell of the leather bindings, the crisp contrast of the black letters against the pure, white page. Many of Michael's books were rare volumes, with watercolors delicately executed on the edges and lithographed illustrations.

My favorite volumes, though, were the anatomy books. I was fascinated by female anatomy, and at one point, I'd begged my husband to train me as a midwife, or as another physician. I'd read about the woman physician, Elizabeth Blackwell, and my own father had been a doctor on the prairie, serving the pioneers as they made their way west. I was not squeamish, could sew a fine stitch, and had a steady grip, but Michael only laughed.

A woman physician, an obstetrician no less! Why, I couldn't be serious! he had roared. Besides, I had enough work being the Angel of his House and the mother of his children. I could doctor them when they had the colic and make potions for Bess when she'd had too much "medicinal" brandy. His wife had no need of work, and ladies of my class stitched fancywork, not bodies.

All this took place before I'd miscarried of the child, miscarried of my savior. My husband seldom took enough notice of me these days to chide me for my unorthodox ideas. He and the specialist suspected that reading and ideas contributed to my delicate nervous condition and caused me to lose his child. So, the study, too, became off-limits.

Michael also suspected that I was too "excited" when I submitted to my wifely duties, a clear sign of dementia and hysteria in a respectable woman. My husband often quoted to me the reputed words of the gracious Queen Victoria whom we all admired for one thing or another, 'lie back, and think of the empire,' as advice. But, I couldn't help it; I suppose I was a harlot at heart, as bad as those he went to relieve his manly desires, those passions too unsuitable to display with one's wife. I, too, had passions, and my husband's touch, his body, no matter how inept, managed to stir them. He and the Chicago specialist consulted again, and they performed an operation on me, one that removed the organ causing my hysterical responses. So, not only was I barren; I could no longer feel. Yet, I did not think of

Victoria's empire; all I thought of what I'd lost, whose fault it all was, and revenge.

Then came the day when my dear husband explained to me that he'd contracted the oldest of diseases from one of the 'girls' some time ago. It certainly was no longer prudent for us to be together. I thought back to the medical books I'd read, and I realized the symptoms Michael had been experiencing dated back a long time, before the child, and I realized that it was he who was responsible for the death of our unborn child, it was he who had made me barren, infected me with his traitorous malady.

Since I'd been treated with mercury periodically, and later with strychnine, I had chills in summer, and constant aches. There were always gray shadows under my eyes, but I'd shown no other symptoms, so the disease was arrested.

I no longer accepted the invitations from Michael's friends and their wives, or from mine for that matter. What would be the point? They all had large families of rosy-cheeked healthy children in imitation of Queen Victoria and her happy brood.

I?

I had failed 'in business.' We had no 'family firm.' Our friends felt awkward around me, hushed. I was never asked to participate in the occasions that marked their children's lives, the weddings, the parties, even the occasional funeral. Within my own circle I became a pitied outsider. Michael attended medical conferences and social gatherings alone, blaming my delicate constitution for my absence.

And I?

I stole away to the study or the nursery whenever I could, and I read. I knew that the malady could drive one mad, and it was only a matter of time, for both of us, but I hoped my time came first.

My husband was home less and less. He took to drinking a lot, and to spending more and more time in the Unfaithful Mermaid and Riverville. Most of the prostitutes and saloon girls, too, were infected, and Michael didn't care if they were. His symptoms were arrested, and he wanted only to carouse among the women of the saloons, to revel in debauchery and lewdness, to give way to the two passions in his life, alcohol and women.

My husband enjoyed the variety in his hunts—he would even travel to the cities or further for the freshest or turning to our small river communities out of necessity. It was this last group that Michael relished the most, as I overheard him more than once telling another of his esteemed colleagues of his adventures, of the thrill of some depraved, louse-ridden creature with ginny breath and rotting teeth. I don't think he ever really saw their faces or knew their names. People who had to sleep in dustbins and doorways often were silent audiences to his trysts, and I don't think they knew their best customer was the esteemed doctor.

It was after overhearing one of these conversations that I conceived of my plan.

My beautiful plan of revenge.

He, and they, had robbed me of my child, of my marriage; they robbed me of my life, so they should lose theirs.

A simple eye for an eye.

Bess had a series of leather butchers aprons she used in the kitchen, and we had a large supply of curettes, scalpels, and knives of all types. The aprons easily covered my clothing, and cheap work clothes were easy to find in the attic and pantry, so I was ready. I learned to steal out at night in the hot, close summer to hunt. Bess would be snoring, Jim Salt would be either out at his mother's, or asleep at the other end of the house.

I had only to wait till my husband left, which was nearly every night. I disguised myself in a work shirt, an old pair of trousers and a cloak of Michael's. He'd told me to discard these, but there was a lot of wear in them. At the time, I thought of the church sales and Christmas boxes for the poor, so I stored them in my trunk. Later, I kept them in the toy box in the nursery, brown and stiff as they were from the blood that escaped the apron when I worked. I had only to wait, to steal out and begin my hunts, my righteous hunts in the name of decent women everywhere.

More and more opportunities came to me as Bess drank more and Michael ignored his home more often. In the chilly autumn evenings, I was able to steal out and revenge myself on Michael, on his despicable secret life, on the whole world. I longed to take trophies as my English soul mate, the Ripper did, and one morning I served my husband what he thought were sheep's kidneys for breakfast. Instead, they were the last remnants of his latest conquest.

As I wrote these last words in my journal, the sun was setting. The shadows elongated the bars forming on the nursery floor. I changed my clothes and prepared myself. I checked my instruments, consulted the brief itinerary I planned for myself. Tonight would be my finale, my masterwork. They would be writing about me for years after this one, maybe I would take up more pages than the British Ripper.

But I had to hurry, the light grew dim and the children of the night awaited me.

The hunt was about to begin.

The ghost finished her story, and she looked at me with big, sad eyes that glowed in her pale face. She looked a little eager, a little pained, as if she wanted my approval, but also as if she felt she had shocked me so badly that I could not give it. For all my terror, I felt some empathy for her. I didn't know if it was for the sadness that motivated her awful crime wave, or the fact that she remained in anonymity.

I think I understood what she wanted of me; I think she wanted me to tell her story. That's why she led me to the trunk, and to the brittle pages of once expensive paper rolled up and stuffed inside the doll's body.

I smiled at her; picked up my laptop, and began to tap on the keys. I still felt her presence in front of me, so I looked up. She was fading away with the morning light, but there was a tinge of a smile on her sad visage (perhaps it was a trick of the light), but I think that she waved to me as she faded away into the cabbage rose wallpaper.

About the Editor

Ellen Tsagaris holds a doctor of philosophy degree in English and literature from Southern Illinois University, a master of arts and juris doctorate from the University of Iowa, and a baccalaureate degree in English and Spanish from Augustana College. She is a college professor, blogger, doll curator and a lifelong poet. *Sappho, I should have listened* is a chapbook of her poetry (2011), and she is the author of *The Subversion of Romance in the Novels of Barbara Pym* (1998) and A *Bibliography of Doll and Toy Sources* (2011).

About Mary Eveline Parkhurst

Mary Eveline Parkhurst was a minister and poet born in LeClaire in 1852, the daughter of Waldo and Liddie Parkhurst, and died June 1927 at the age of 75 years old. She was known to the people of Scott County as a poetess and published *The Citadel of Thought* (1917) immortalizing the Green Tree and the Mississippi River, and gave council in verse to the German nation. She taught for a number of years at School #1 in LeClaire Township and LeClaire. She was also the the author of "Sketch of LeClaire" published in Davenport for the *Half-Century Democrat. (from Our Story: Bridging the Past and the Present)*

About the Ghost Story Writers

Theresa Davis is a former president and secretary/treasurer of the Romance Writers of the Quad Cities, an affiliate of Romance Writers of America. Her editorials have appeared in *The Moline Dispatch* and *The Rock Island Argus* and she works as an inventory manager for Group O Companies, Supply Chain Solutions Division. She holds a black belt in Kuk Sool Won, a Korean martial art, and is a licensed Zumba instructor. She lives with her husband Patrick, a big dog, and a cat.

Darren Hall is an English teacher at Geneseo High School, is a past winner of a ghost story and fishing tale contest sponsored by *The Rock Island Argus*, and a past guest columnist for the *Argus*.

Steven Lackey was born in 1949 and has been writing and drawing comic strips since 1955. His *SUPER-HERO UNION LOCAL #1* was an award-winning comic strip that ran for two years in QCA newspapers. He has won several awards at the Mississippi Valley Writers Conference, and serves as president of the Writers Studio in Davenport. He is the author of the graphic novel, *Artist Wanted* (2011).

Jannette LaRoche is a native Quad Citian and resides in East Moline. She is a graduate of United Township High School, Black Hawk College, Northern Illinois University, and the Graduate School of Library and Information Science at the University of Illinois. She is a reference and teens services librarian at the Moline Public Library.

Heide Larson began her career as education coordinator for eastern Iowa Head Start programs, following which she taught preschool and college classes in the area for 15 years. During her 10 years on the sales staff of Borders Books & Music in Davenport, she conducted literacy activities for children of all ages. Today, Heide manages a meal service for seniors in LeClaire and Princeton through the Area Agency on Aging. She professes, "writing is my muse and defense against age-related cognitive impairment."

Ron Leiby is an Illinois native, has lived in LeClaire since 1974, and is retired from Qwest Communications after 35 years in the telecommunications field. He serves on the Board of Directors of the Buffalo Bill Museum, and has represented LeClaire for 30 years as a Democratic Precinct Committee Representative. He is a graduate of Eastern Iowa Community College, a U.S. Navy Vietnam veteran, and a past mayor and councilman for the city of LeClaire having served 12 years as councilman. Ron is an avid community volunteer having served on the board of directors for the LeClaire Jaycees, LeClaire Community Association of Volunteers, LeClaire "Buffalo Bill" Post 347 American Legion, Scott County American Legion, and LeClaire Civic Club. He serves on the Scott County Condemnation Review Board, and has also served on the Scott County 911 Service Board.

Rose Richardson has lived in LeClaire for 36 years, and is currently employed at the Pleasant Valley School District. She serves as a volunteer for the Buffalo Bill Museum.

Debbie Smith has lived in LeClaire for 36 years and is recently retired from the Department of Defense at Rock Island Arsenal. She is the current President of the Buffalo Bill Museum and continues to enjoy learning the history of LeClaire.

Janet Willman has lived in LeClaire for 28 years, and serves on the Board of the Buffalo Bill Museum as treasurer. She is retired after 32 years as a Department of Defense accountant at the Rock Island Arsenal.

Connie (Corcoran) Wilson of East Moline has written professionally for 56 years for five newspapers and nine blogs, and taught junior high school language arts, writing and literature classes at all six Quad City area colleges. She has published five short story collections, two novels, two books of humorous essays, and one illustrated children's book via six different publishers. Her short story collection, *Hellfire & Damnation*, finished in seventh out of 46 entries on the preliminary balloting for the Bram Stoker award in 2011, three places ahead of eventual winner, Stephen King's *Full Dark, No Stars*. The sequel, *Hellfire & Damnation II*, will be released in 2012. She is a member of the Midwest Writing Center (2010 David R. Collins Writer of the Year), the Illinois Women's Press Association, Midwest Writers Association for non-fiction writers, American Writing Program (AWP), ThrillerWriters, and the Horror Writers' Association (HWA). She blogs for Yahoo as a featured writer for politics, television and movies and has blogged for the 600,000 member Associated Content, which named her its 2008 Content Producer of the Year, for www.blogforiowa.com and for her own blog, www.WeeklyWilson.com. Her latest release is the novel, *The Color of Evil* (Quad Cities Press, 2012).